Julian's fi... brought a profound shock. Was this truly Pamela, his childhood companion? He could not recall ever seeing her in anything other than an old gown as she sat by his side fishing or scampered through the woods with him. Was this the girl who had said she cared nothing for her appearance? The girl he had called plain?

For she wasn't plain. Not dressed in a new and fashionable gown of pale-blue muslin, her hair cropped and curled, her eyes sparkling with mischief at something Miss Winley had said.

Miss Winley! Abruptly Julian realized that his thoughts ought to be on her. He hastily stepped forward to greet her. Both ladies noticed him at the same moment.

As for Pamela, had she seen the way Julian looked at her the moment before, it might have brightened her spirits. But she only saw how resolutely he made his way straight for Miss Winley. . . .

Miss Tibbles Investigates

April Kihlstrom

A SIGNET BOOK

SIGNET
Published by New American Library, a division of
Penguin Putnam Inc., 375 Hudson Street,
New York, New York 10014, U.S.A.
Penguin Books Ltd, 27 Wrights Lane,
London W8 5TZ, England
Penguin Books Australia Ltd, Ringwood,
Victoria, Australia
Penguin Books Canada Ltd, 10 Alcorn Avenue,
Toronto, Ontario, Canada M4V 3B2
Penguin Books (N.Z.) Ltd, 182–190 Wairau Road,
Auckland 10, New Zealand

Penguin Books Ltd, Registered Offices:
Harmondsworth, Middlesex, England

First published by Signet, an imprint of New American Library,
a division of Penguin Putnam Inc.

First Printing, June 2000
10 9 8 7 6 5 4 3 2 1

PUBLISHER'S NOTE
This is a work of fiction. Names, characters, places, and incidents either
are the product of the author's imagination or are used fictitiously,
and any resemblance to actual persons, living or dead, business
establishments, events, or locales is entirely coincidental.

Characters

First Earl of Kendall

(by 1st wife)   (by 2nd wife)

Second Earl (67) [& Countess (60)] Kendall   Lady Gwendolyn (51) (& Mr. Avery)

Harry (died in duel) & Edward, Lord Fairchild (41) [& Anna (35)]   Daphne (33) & Richard (35)

Pamela (16)   3 brothers, youngest in nursery

Lord and Lady Winley

Catherine (19)

Julian Deerwood (20) (eldest son of a baron)

Mrs. Merriweather (Miss Tibbles) (40) & Colonel Merriweather (45)

Chapter 1

Pamela Fairchild, granddaughter of the Earl of Kendall, stared at her childhood playmate, Julian Deerwood. They had scrambled through the woods together as children, landed in the pond more than once, scraped mud off each other, and even patched up each other's cuts and bruises when they tumbled out of a tree a time or two. At the moment they were seated side by side, in their oldest clothes, each one holding a fishing pole. It was just as it had always been. Except that Julian was all grown up: tall and slender, with deep brown eyes, brown hair fashionably cropped, and he planned to be married. Or so he said.

"Miss Winley has accepted your suit, then?" Pamela asked with some constraint as she set aside her pole.

Julian looked away. "Not precisely," he admitted. "Her father has forbidden me to offer for her."

"But then surely—" Pamela broke off as she saw the unhappiness cloud her friend's face. As she had always done, she entered into the spirit of things despite her own doubts. "How do you mean to contrive the thing, then? Elope to Gretna Green?"

"If she would have me, why, then yes," Julian answered defiantly. Apparently, however, he read the reproach in Pamela's eyes for he lowered his own and said, more tamely, "I have hopes that Lord Winley will come about. Once he sees that the affection his daughter and I have for each other is constant, he may give his consent. He must! After all, he claimed to forbid the match on the grounds that we were both too young."

Pamela was too wise to tell Julian that she was inclined to agree with Lord Winley. Instead she plucked at the fabric of her skirt as she said, "Six months ago you said you never meant to marry. She must be very beautiful to have changed your mind so quickly."

"She is!"

Julian agreed with a fervor that Pamela found most distressing. Still she persisted. "I suppose she looks nothing like me."

"Oh, no," Julian agreed again, oblivious to the distress he was causing his friend. "She is delicate, not sturdy like you. And her hair is angelically fair, unlike your brown curls, while her eyes are blue, not green. Her complexion has never, I should think, been marred by her spending too much time in the sun."

He paused and regarded Pamela critically. "I shouldn't think one would ever catch her fishing at a pond in her oldest dress! Indeed, I think her family must have taken the greatest care of her all these years. It is precisely her beauty that makes her mother aim higher than the son of a baron, even if I am the heir," he concluded with a disconsolate note to his voice. "She will be the harder one to convince."

"Well, if Miss Winley cares for you as much as you say she does," Pamela told Julian stoutly as she touched his arm in reassurance, "then she will refuse all offers, no matter how noble the suitor, and wait for you."

"I wish I may believe it," Deerwood said with a sigh. "But if I am here and she is in London, I fear she may forget me."

That, Pamela thought privately, must be impossible if the girl had even a bit of a heart. But she did not say so aloud. Instead she said, "You told me you had a favor to ask. What was it, Julian?"

He turned to her, hope in his eyes. "Will you invite her to come to Kendall Hall to stay? For at least a fortnight? That would give me time to fix myself more firmly in her heart and then together perhaps we could persuade her father to change his mind."

"But I do not even know Miss Winley," Pamela said, taken aback.

"Oh, you will adore her!" Julian said with the certainty only a man could or would bring to the situation. "And I suppose she will like you too for you are a very good girl. Certainly a very sensible one."

Pamela bit her tongue to keep from answering as she wished. "I meant that Miss Winley is most unlikely to accept an invitation from someone she does not know. Nor are her parents likely to let her accept."

Julian waved away her objections with an impatient gesture. "No, you do not understand. Lady Winley is absurdly ambitious for Catherine. She will be grateful for the chance for her daughter to stay in the home of an earl. Tell her your brothers wish to meet her."

"My brothers are at Eton, except Paul, who is in the nursery."

"Lady Winley need not know that! Look, Pamela, I have told her about you, about my scheme, for I made sure you would agree and she will know to accept and pretend that you have some chance acquaintance between you."

With a greater reluctance than she would admit, even to herself, Pamela agreed to invite Miss Catherine Winley to Kendall Hall. And if she privately prayed that the young lady or her parents would refuse the invitation, well, she was far too wise and kind to say so aloud to Julian. Her reward was that he took his leave of her with a brotherly kiss on her forehead.

"And do try to acquire some new clothes before she comes," he told Pamela briskly. "She is accustomed to London society and one wouldn't want her to think you dowdy. I know you're the best of girls but people do go on appearances and at the moment you scarcely look like a lady."

Just why that left her feeling even more disconsolate than before, Pamela could not have said. It was not as though she had any vanity. Too many years of being told by her grandmother that she lacked any social graces and was dreadfully plain had long since cured her of hoping she would ever have any pretensions to beauty. Mama, of course, stoutly denied Grandmama's charges, but Julian's words had just confirmed them.

She was not, Pamela admitted to herself, looking forward to meeting the young woman who had won Julian's heart. But she had promised she would invite Catherine Winley to visit and she would do her best to do so. Now all she had to do was convince Mama.

Back at Kendall Hall, in the library, Lady Fairchild's mind was on another matter entirely than the question of houseguests, though she did have her own invitation she meant to extend. But for now she regarded her husband with some concern. He seemed scarcely aware of her presence and she did her needlework silently, not wishing to remind him she was here. Still, it worried her that he sighed and looked off into the fireplace, and then took the same packet of letters out and read them through all over again, for perhaps the third time today.

If only she knew where he kept those letters! She had looked, more than once, when Fairchild was away from the room, and been unable to find them. Somehow, somewhere, he kept them hidden and that alone was enough to worry her. She wished she knew what they contained.

On the desk was her own letter, waiting to be franked by her father-in-law, the Earl of Kendall. She bit her lower lip, wondering if she should remind her husband. But when he was in this mood, she did not dare. Still, the sooner it went out, the better she would feel.

So worried was she, so prepared for the worst, that Lady Fairchild did not even flinch when Lord Fairchild suddenly took his glass of brandy and flung it into the fireplace so that it shattered and sent the flames roaring even higher.

"What the devil are you doing in here?" he shouted at her.

With a tranquillity she was far from feeling, Lady Fairchild answered, "Merely doing my needlework, as I always have, here in the library with you."

"Well, don't do it anymore!" he snarled. "You distract me. Go and sit with my mother or something."

Gathering her things together, and trying very hard to conceal the distress that threatened to completely overset her composure, Lady Fairchild swept out of the room, her back rigidly straight and her head held high. She would not, after twenty years of marriage, allow him to humiliate her now. She did, however, retrieve the letter from the desk, where she had placed it a day or two before. She herself, it seemed, would have to ask Lord Kendall to frank it.

It did not occur to her to flee to her room. That would have been cowardly and Lady Fairchild was never a coward. Instead she did as he had asked and found her mother-in-law, Lady Kendall, sitting by the fire in the drawing room. She was sitting with Lord Kendall's sister, Lady Gwendolyn Avery, and neither looked particularly happy.

That may have been due, in part, to the presence of Lord Fairchild's cousins. Richard Avery was a particularly rackety young man who, at five-and-thirty, showed no signs of settling down. His sister, Daphne Avery, at three-and-thirty was a confirmed spinster and one who was patently not happy with her state. Their discontented faces alone could have accounted for the ill-humor in the room.

But Lady Fairchild knew it did not. "Where is Papa?" she asked, in her gentle way.

Without looking up, Lady Kendall answered her. "Kendall is out hunting, I suppose. He usually is, at this time of day."

"He would be even if it was pouring rain, which it isn't," Richard Avery chimed in. "Uncle hasn't the slightest particle of sense when it comes to such things."

"I've no sense?" a voice demanded from the doorway.

They all turned to look, of course, and the gentleman standing there smiled with a sort of sour satisfaction. Then and only then did he slowly advance into the room.

Although he had almost seventy years in his dish, Lord Kendall was still a fine-looking man and one who had the energy of many a man half his age. He stood as straight, dressed with as much care, as if he were years younger. Now his eyes bored into the young man in the room.

"You," he said, "have far too much of that sort of sense and I pity you for it!"

Avery flushed. He muttered something but only his sister could hear what he said.

Kendall snorted with disgust. "That's right, whisper it! You're too much of a coward to confront me, much less Boney's men."

"The war is over, Uncle!" Daphne said timidly, in her brother's defense.

"I know that," Kendall snapped back. "But even when it wasn't, your brother wouldn't let me buy him a commission. Pity. It's the one thing that might have made a real man of him."

Avery straightened. He took a step toward his uncle. "What you mean is that it's a pity I didn't go off to war and get myself killed, don't you?" he asked.

Kendall shrugged. "Oh, give over, boy. I meant nothing of the sort! I just wish you would take up some sort of occupation. Manage your cousin's estate or marry and manage your own," he said impatiently.

Avery flushed again. But his back was still straight and his voice steady as he replied, "It has never been my desire to manage the affairs of another. Nor will I marry without the means to support a wife. My father made that mistake and it is one I shall not copy."

The earl nodded. There was a grudging respect in his voice as he said, "Aye, there is some sense to that, I suppose. Your father was a damned fool. But you could marry, if you married someone with money. All that's required is that you make yourself agreeable to the girl. Plenty of 'em about, looking for husbands. What with the war and all, there aren't nearly enough eligible young men about. Just ask Daphne. Eh, girl?"

It was her turn to flush. However, she turned away and refused to be drawn into matters. Only Lady Fairchild saw how tightly her hands gripped the sides of the chair she sat in, how stiffly she held herself.

Wishing to divert her father-in-law's attention, Lady Fairchild drew the letter from her pocket.

"Will you frank this for me, Papa?" she asked.

"Who's it to?" he demanded, even as he took the thing.

"Miss Tibbles. My former governess," Lady Fairchild explained. "She is Mrs. Merriweather now. Married to a Colonel Merriweather. I thought I would ask her to come for a short visit."

That stopped all conversation in the room, as she had known it would. They all stared at her and Lady Fairchild felt the color in her cheeks rising.

"Ask your old governess for a visit?" Lady Kendall echoed in accents of disbelief. "I have never heard of such a thing! Ridiculous!"

Lady Fairchild tilted her chin upward, just enough that those who had known her in her salad days would have remembered how willful she had once been accounted. Now her voice was gentle but implacable as she said, "Mrs. Merriweather is perfectly respectable. Indeed, she is a lady now. No one need think anything of it if you do not tell them what she once was. They will only think we have a charming woman staying with us."

The others looked at one another, as Lady Fairchild knew they would, and exchanged speaking glances. Finally Lady Gwendolyn said with a distinct sniff, "Just so long as you do not expect us to entertain her!"

At the thought of Miss Tibbles expecting to be entertained, Lady Fairchild smiled wryly to herself. But she must remember, it was Mrs. Merriweather now.

Aloud she said, "I shan't and neither shall she."

"Doubtful," Lord Kendall said briskly. "Encroaching. All these sorts of people are. But do as you will. I told you when Edward brought you here as a bride that you were to treat this house as if it were your own home. Meant it. So have this woman here for a visit if you wish. Give me her direction and I shall see that this goes in the very next post."

Lady Fairchild could not help herself. Impulsively she rose to her feet and crossed the short distance to Lord Kendall. She put a hand on his arm and said warmly, "Thank you, Papa! You have always made me feel welcome here and I am very grateful to you for it."

He smiled and chuckled. "Yes, well, you're a good puss. And you've given Edward four pledges of your affection. Three fine, healthy boys and a daughter. So you've rewarded us four times over for any kindness we may have shown you."

Lady Kendall rose to her feet now and came over beside Lady Fairchild. She put an arm around her and said, as warmly as the earl, "It is quite true! You have been the best daughter I could have wished for. So if you wish this woman to come, then come she shall, however odd we may think such a visit to be. The letter shall be sent at once. Now come and sit and tell us how our grandsons are doing. Have you had any letters from them at Eton?"

Lady Fairchild allowed herself to be led to a seat by the fire and distracted by talk of her children. She accounted herself fortunate to be in a household that loved children so well and wished to hear of the exploits of her darlings. Still, at the back of her mind was the memory of Edward staring at the letters and flinging his glass of brandy into the fireplace. Somehow she had to discover what was going on!

In the library, Lord Fairchild felt the bile rise into his throat, a circumstance that was happening with alarming regularity these days.

But he didn't bother to consult a doctor. What was the point? He knew where the trouble lay. It lay in these letters, here on his desk. Letters that if he had the slightest bit of sense he would burn. Letters he could not bear to part with.

Anna, he thought, suspected them to be love letters. He knew she did and he could not blame her. Nor did he try to disabuse her of her mistake. Far better she believe that than have her guess the truth.

No, he loved Anna and he had sworn to protect her. He would do his best, at whatever cost, to continue to do so, until the day he died. What worried him the most was that he no longer was certain he was capable of doing so. And that was what woke him in the night.

A clock chimed somewhere in the house and with a start Lord Fairchild realized the time. He would have to go up and change for dinner at once. Mama did not like it when anyone was late to dinner, and besides, he had been attracting enough strange glances from his family, of late, without making matters any worse.

He rose to his feet and crossed the room to make certain the door was locked and a piece of cloth stuck in the keyhole to prevent anyone peeking in. Overly cautious, perhaps, but Fairchild couldn't risk anyone finding and reading these letters.

Only when he was certain he was safe from both interruption and prying eyes did he move to his secret hiding place. And with a heavy heart he placed the letters inside.

Lord Fairchild was no closer to a solution to his dilemma than he had been when he entered the room three hours earlier. Indeed, he was no closer than when the first letter arrived, two months before.

He accounted himself an intelligent man, but no matter how he turned his mind to the situation, he could see no way out of disaster. Nor could he see any way to keep Anna from growing increasingly suspicious.

Well, unless divine providence intervened in the form of a miracle, soon the entire world would know his secret and nothing would matter anymore.

Fairchild retrieved the piece of cloth and unlocked the door. Swiftly he headed up the stairs to his dressing room. Disaster might be about to strike, but he still must dress for dinner and play out the part assigned to him until the very end.

Fortunately his valet was waiting with everything laid out to be donned in haste. In the other room he could hear Anna moving about and he felt again her unhappiness, even without being able to see her face.

He resolved to dress with even greater haste and managed to finish in time to catch her before she left her room. She was reaching for the door to the hallway when he opened the one between their rooms.

"Anna," he said, then stopped.

She looked at him and stiffened, as if bracing herself for what he might say. It tore at him and he reached out a hand.

"I thought we might go down together," he said.

She hesitated only a moment, then nodded. He saw her swallow hard then come toward him, and as she placed her hand in his, he could see it tremble. Still she did place it in his and he closed his hand around hers tightly.

For a moment, just a moment, he wished he could confide in her. But that was impossible. And instead, he cleared his throat and said, "We'd best go down."

She nodded and began to talk of little things about the house. Fairchild thanked the heavens for her good sense.

Chapter 2

Miss Catherine Winley stared at the letter she held. Then she looked at her mother. How could she accomplish her goal? After a moment, she smiled a smile her mother would greatly have distrusted had she seen it. Fortunately, her mother's face was turned away from her.

"Mama?" Catherine all but purred as she spoke.

"Yes, dear?"

"Miss Fairchild has invited us to come for a visit to her country home."

Mrs. Winley frowned. "I do not recall meeting a Fairchild. Was it at Lady Jersey's ball?"

"Oh, no. Miss Fairchild is someone I met at school," Catherine said with a false yawn. "I do not say I wish to go, I am merely telling you about the invitation. I daresay it would be a dead bore. She is the grand-daughter of the Earl of Kendall, and while she has three brothers, I am persuaded none of them could be of interest to us."

Her mother's eyes opened wide, as Catherine knew they would. "Three brothers?"

"Yes, but I've no interest in any of them," Catherine said with perfect truth.

"Catherine," her mother said, in a tone that would brook no refusal, "you will write Miss Fairchild and tell her we should be delighted to come for a visit. How soon does she ask us to come?"

* * *

Mrs. Merriweather, born Marian Elizabeth Tibbles, stared at the letter in her hand. Across the breakfast table, her husband, Colonel Merriweather, frowned.

"Trouble?" he asked.

"Not precisely," Marian replied. "Indeed, it is a very kind invitation from Lady Fairchild to come and stay with her. She was the very first girl given into my charge when I became a governess. She was fifteen years to my twenty when I came there, and a sweet child, if a trifle impulsive. That was twenty years ago, of course, so it is very kind of her to remember me at all and even more so to extend me this invitation."

"But?" Merriweather asked. "I know that look of yours. Something is troubling you."

Marian sighed. "But I fear something is wrong. Although she wrote to me after our wedding, it seems strange to receive such an invitation so suddenly."

"Perhaps it is because she remembers you with fondness and now that you are a respectable lady rather than a governess she feels she can ask you to visit?" Merriweather suggested. "Either that or she has need of a governess for her own daughter and hopes to persuade you to the task?"

It was a jest, but it fell sadly flat. Marian knew something was wrong. Still, she considered the first part of what he had said.

"Perhaps it is my new status as your wife," she acknowledged, "and yet I have been for some time now. And there is an urgency to this invitation that argues there is more to it than that. Do you know Lord Fairchild? Or his father, the Earl of Kendall?"

"No. Should I?"

Instead of answering, Marian tapped her chin. "When Anna was married, I recall her father looking into the family. Fairchild's brother, the heir, was accounted something of a wastrel, but Fairchild himself was a gentle, respectable fellow and the brother died a few years after their wedding. In general, the entire family was considered most respectable. What, then, could be troubling her, I wonder."

Amused, the colonel smiled and said, "Why don't you go and see?"

"What about Elizabeth?"

"Take her with you. Bound to be a nursery. They're not likely to object to one more child in it." When she still hesitated, the colonel set down his knife and fork and leaned toward his wife. "Go on, accept the invitation. You know you will only fret yourself if you don't go. I shall manage perfectly well for a week or two."

"How do you know it won't be longer?" Marian asked playfully.

His eyes twinkled as he replied, "Because I know you will not be able to bear being away from me any longer than you must be."

Marian smiled and hesitated no longer. She rose to her feet and said, "Yes, I think I shall go. Lady Fairchild says to come at once. I shall write her and say I am leaving the day after tomorrow."

Colonel Merriweather fondly watched his wife leave the room. For a tuppence he would go with her, but there were some matters that needed attending to here at home. Ah, well, if she wasn't home in a reasonable length of time, he would just have to go and fetch her back. But he had no real fears on that score. He meant it when he said he knew she would not want to be away long. Even after almost two years of marriage they both still felt like newlyweds. It was, he thought, a very nice feeling indeed.

Julian looked at Pamela and at the letter she held in her hand. She was smiling. Surely that was a good sign? "Is she coming?" he asked.

"Oh, yes. Two days from now," Pamela answered, an odd note to her voice. "It seems that she and her

mother are delighted to come and stay at Kendall
Hall. Just as you predicted they would be."

"Excellent!" Julian exclaimed. At his friend's doubtful
expression he took her hands in his. "You will adore
Miss Winley, I know you will. No one could fail to do
so. She is lovely and kind and of the sweetest temperament.
You will find you both suit as friends admirably."

For a long moment, Pamela did not answer and
Julian began to fear she would not, that something
was distressing her. There was a flush of pink that
stole across her cheeks and she could not meet his
eyes. Instead she stared at his hands holding hers, and
almost Julian let go.

But he did not and she said, with the cheerfulness
he associated with her, "Yes, of course I shall like
Miss Winley. It will be very nice to have a young lady
of my own age for companionship during her visit."

Julian so far forgot himself as to give Pamela a
quick hug. And why she should object, when she never
had before, was beyond him. Still, he was far too
happy to worry about it. He chalked it up to feminine
inconstancy and thought no more about the matter.
Instead, as he told her, he was off to arrange some
entertainment for Miss Winley while she was a guest
at Kendall Hall.

"For I am certain," he told Pamela firmly, "that my
mother will have no objection to sending invitations
to dinner and a small, informal entertainment afterwards."

Pamela doubted it. Julian's mother was a very dear
lady but her indifferent health made entertaining more
than she could manage. Indeed, she could not remember
the last time Julian's parents had held a dinner
party or any other social event at their home. But she
said none of this aloud to her friend. Instead Pamela
let him go with a spoken wish that it might be so.

"You are the best of fellows!" Julian told her cheerfully. "Stap me if you're not. Just remember to get yourself some new gowns. I won't have Catherine or her mother thinking your family dowdy. She's a year or two older than you and has much more polish. P'rhaps she can give you a hint or two."

And then he left, not even noticing the tiny tear that trickled down Pamela's cheek as he hurried out the door. If he had noticed, Julian would have been greatly troubled by the sight. He did not like to see anyone in distress and much less so his childhood companion.

There were moments when Julian looked at Pamela and saw the young woman beneath the old dresses she wore and the smudge of dirt that always seemed to be found on her nose and thought how much she had grown up while he was away. At those times he felt a tug of something more than brotherly affection. But that would have been disloyal to Miss Winley, to Catherine, and so he always ruthlessly suppressed it.

Lady Kendall looked at her husband. "Has he offered to confide in you?"

Lord Kendall shook his head. "And you?" he countered. "Has he told you anything?"

"So far as I can discover, he has not even confided in his wife," she said with a sigh.

The earl snorted his disgust. "Damned odd thing if he did! Not that I'm saying she's not a good gel, but a naive little thing she is and not the sort one would tell one's troubles to, I should think."

The countess gently set down her hairbrush and turned to face her husband. "Perhaps. But it worries me. Something is troubling Edward and I cannot think what it might be. Perhaps he would talk to you? Indeed, I am surprised he has not done so already. He always used to come to you with his problems."

The earl looked away. "Yes, well," he said gruffly,

"Edward is a grown man now. I cannot blame him if he wishes to keep his own counsel."

But the countess would not let it go. "In general I would agree," she said, her voice firm, "but this time I am truly worried about Edward. I think, my dear, you shall have to ask what is troubling him."

The earl shook his head in denial, but after a moment, he said, a hint of a sly smile on his face, "Very well, but only if we approach him together. He's always found it easier to talk to you than to me."

She wondered what the smile meant. It made her uneasy. But the countess took his words for both the accolade and the apology that they were. Silently she rose to her feet and gave her husband her hand. He knew, she thought, more than he was telling. But years of marriage had taught her that it was of no use to attempt to pry it out of him. She could only hope he would not find a way to keep her from finding out what was troubling Edward.

"Best we do it now, while the others are dressing for dinner and we may be certain of being uninterrupted while we speak to him."

The earl nodded and together they went in search of their son.

But the earl and countess were mistaken. Daphne and Richard Avery were already in the drawing room. They might well have interrupted the conversation, if they had known or cared that it was taking place.

They had their own concerns.

"Are you certain?" Daphne asked anxiously.

He nodded, his face very pale. "I saw the letters myself, before he could hide them."

She took a turn about the room, trying to compose herself before she tried to answer.

Finally she turned and confronted her brother. "But you don't know for certain what they say. Or when they were written, do you?"

He shook his head. "No. But they ain't years old, if that's what you're hinting."

Her hands began to tremble and she hid them in the folds of her skirt. Richard came to stand beside her and put an arm around her shoulders. Softly he said, "You're safe now, Daphne. I swear it. I'll do whatever it takes to protect you, this time around."

In reply, Daphne could only turn and stare up at him with large, shimmering brown eyes. "And who," she asked softly, "will protect you?"

In the kitchen there was grumbling over the fact that dinner had been set back twice.

"Done right to a turn, they was," the cook's chief assistant said, pointing to the capons on a spit over the fire. "Overdone, more like, now."

"Bloody family don't never stop to think about such things," one of the footman spat. "But it'll be us what gets the complaints if they don't like the food."

"Here, now! That's enough of such talk!" Damford, the butler, snapped. "You, Peters, upstairs now. And the rest of you, look lively. The family means to dine in half an hour and everything had best be ready."

If there were further protests, they were carried on so softly that Damford couldn't hear. But his nose twitched nevertheless. Eighteen years in this household had taught him to know when trouble was brewing. And if ever it had, it was brewing right now. Damford didn't like that, he didn't like it one bit.

Nice and smooth, that's how he liked things to run. And for as long as he could make them do so, he would.

The housekeeper came to stand beside him. "In a taking, are they, abovestairs?" she asked in a voice pitched so low that only he could hear.

He ought to have depressed her with a word, sent her on her way without the slightest encouragement. But they had been friends too long. Indeed, there had even been a time he had considered marrying her. But he had tarried too long and another man wooed and won her.

Still they were friends and accustomed to sharing each other's confidences. "Not so's you could put your finger on it," he answered. "Not so much so that anyone from outside the family would guess. But we've been here far too long, Mrs. Breen, not to notice the way they're looking at one another. Nor the way they're speaking, so careful like, around the staff. Mark my words, Mrs. Breen, there'll be trouble here, and before too much more time passes, I'd say."

She didn't contradict him. That was one of the nice things about Mrs. Breen. She looked up to Damford, she did. Never questioned his authority like some of the pert young things about the place.

No, Mrs. Breen merely nodded sagely and said, "Well, it's a comfort to me, it is, Mr. Damford, and a comfort to the family as well, I'll be bound, to have you looking out for them."

"Why thank you, Mrs. Breen," he said, a little taken aback by the compliment. "And I know that Lady Kendall depends upon you."

The housekeeper's face softened into the lines of a smile. "Aye, that she does," Mrs. Breen said softly. "That she does. And I won't never let her down, I won't. No more'n you'll ever let down his lordship neither, will you? You'd do anything for this family, same as I would, I'll be bound."

But this familiarity was too much for Damford. Particularly as they were beginning to draw the curious glances of other servants, some of whom were trying to find excuses to come and stand close enough to overhear.

So now Damford said in a repressive voice, taking a step away from the housekeeper, "That will be all, Mrs. Breen. I must go up and make certain all is ready for their dinner."

Too wise to protest, she merely watched him go.

*   *   *

Lady Gwendolyn Avery stood outside the drawing room door. The voices of her children, Daphne and Richard, had fallen so soft that she could no longer overhear what they were saying. Her own expression twisted into something akin to a snarl and she moved along the hallway to the library. If she were quick about it, perhaps she could find what she was looking for before the others came down for dinner.

Her velvet gown scarcely rustled as she moved. That was by choice. No fool, Lady Gwendolyn was well aware that she would have no excuse if she were to be caught. But there was no reason she should be.

The servants would all be in the kitchen at this hour, or the dining room, preparing for the family meal. The family, aside from the Avery children, would be getting changed. No, it should be safe enough. If she were quick. But she must not, she told herself, count on having more than ten minutes to do what she must do.

The moment the library door was locked behind her, Lady Gwendolyn moved over to the desk and began pulling open drawers. Nothing! Nothing that was of any use to her at any rate.

Five minutes gone and still nothing found.

Lady Gwendolyn gripped the edge of the desk and looked around. There must be some other place that things could be hidden, but where?

She felt along the mantelpiece. Nothing. She looked swiftly over at the bookcases. There were hundreds of books on the shelves and anything could be hidden in any one of them. She would never have time to search them all. Perhaps a few, at random?

Even as she hesitated, the doorknob rattled. She froze. Then, slowly, she walked toward the door, growing more composed with each step. She had, after all, faced this sort of thing before.

A turn of the key, a small cry of surprise at the sight of her nephew, Lord Fairchild.

"Edward, I am so sorry. I wanted only a moment of sanctuary here alone, and did not think anyone else would need to come in just now," she said.

He smiled, warmly, at her. "It is all right, Aunt Gwendolyn. I quite understand. Do you wish to be alone a little longer?"

She reached up and patted his cheek. "Dear boy! No, I am feeling much better now and I must suppose the others are already waiting in the drawing room. Had you come in search of me to say I was late?"

He hesitated and Lady Gwendolyn knew he was about to deny it. But then he changed his mind and said, "Yes, of course. I knew you would not wish to be late."

He offered her his arm and she took it. How could she not? To do otherwise would be to force words to be spoken that would put the lie to both of them. And that, of course, would never do.

Chapter 3

As the carriage swept down the drive, Mrs. Merriweather surveyed the imposing household before
her. Kendall Hall resembled a castle more than a
country manor house, albeit a very small one. Since
she knew it was no more than fifty years old, she
could only conclude that the man who had built it,
the previous Earl of Kendall, somehow thought that
olden times were far more romantic than the present.

Mind you, one would expect an earl to have an
imposing residence, perhaps even a genuine castle to
go along with the title. Such families, after all, tended
to have a long provenance.

The first Earl of Kendall, however, had received his
title only fifty-five years before, along with the land
and funds to build this home. No one quite knew what
service he had rendered the crown to jump so precipitously from unknown commoner to earl, but he had
done so, nonetheless. And then died a year after moving into this place. The current Earl of Kendall and
his son had apparently seen no need to alter any of
the original plans.

Still, it was a well-staffed household, and before the
carriage even came to a halt, the front door was
opened and an imposing major domo waited to announce her.

But Marian would not be hurried. She made certain
little Elizabeth was still asleep, then directed her maid
to take the baby straight up to the nursery. And told

her, for no doubt the hundredth time, what orders the woman was to give the servants there.

Only when she was done did Marian allow the coachman to help her down. And she waited for the maid before she began to climb the steps to the front door. That was her first mistake, for another carriage swept up the drive and pulled to a halt right behind hers. The ladies inside that carriage made no delay in emerging and, with one dismissive look, immediately moved ahead of her to mount the steps.

The major domo looked at the other ladies and then at Marian and promptly bowed to the other ladies. Suddenly the smile that had noticeably been absent when he looked at her was granted to those ladies. Marian began to conceive a strong dislike for both them and the major domo. That led to her second mistake.

She climbed the steps, her maid at her side, and defiantly came to stand next to the two ladies. The elder one looked Marian up and down and then said, "The servants' entrance is to the rear, I should think." And to the major domo the lady added, "Indeed, it is a sad trial these days trying to find properly trained people."

Marian bristled visibly. In a deceptively calm voice, however, she said, "You surely cannot expect me to have my maid bring my child around to the rear?"

"Your maid?" the lady echoed skeptically.

"Yes, mine. I am Mrs. Merriweather. Colonel Merriweather's wife."

The other woman appeared startled, but only for a moment. She apparently concluded that a mere colonel's wife could be of little account to her because she turned to her daughter and said, "Catherine, it is cool out here and I should not wish you to catch a chill."

And without any apology for her rudeness, the older woman swept into Kendall Hall, followed by the younger woman, bowed in by the major domo. He allowed Marian to follow but cast a look of profound distaste at the sight of the baby. Marian stared him down.

"Lady Fairchild no doubt forgot to mention that I would be bringing my daughter. If you will have some-one show my maid to the nursery, it would be a wise notion. Before my daughter wakes."

The major domo, who had been at the household through the infancy of several Fairchild children, made haste to do as he was bid. And by then Lady Fairchild herself was all but running down the stairs.

"Miss Tibbles! How wonderful of you to come!"

"I am quite certain, Anna, that I taught you better than to come running down the stairs!" Mrs. Merri-weather said.

She meant to be stern, but there was so much soft-ness in the older woman's gaze that Lady Fairchild was not in the least deceived. She gave a little gurgle of laughter that reminded her former governess of the girl she once had been.

"Of course you did!" Lady Fairchild said unrepen-tantly. "But how could I not run to see my dear Miss Tibbles? Though I must call you Mrs. Merriweather now, must I not? It seems so strange!"

"That I should be married?" Mrs. Merriweather asked in quelling tones.

"No, that you should be here at all," Lady Fairchild answered, holding out her hands.

Mrs. Merriweather took them, though she ought not to have done so. It was far too familiar a gesture be-tween the wife of a future earl and a former governess. Still she took them and squeezed just as hard as Lady Fairchild did.

"How do you go on, my dear?" she asked, a wealth of emotion in those few words.

Damford cleared his throat, reminding them both

that he was still there. Lady Fairchild abruptly stilled and slowly pulled her hands free.

"You must be tired after your journey," Lady Fairchild said in a cool, brisk voice, entirely appropriate to her station.

"Yes, I suppose I am," Mrs. Merriweather conceded. "Might we go into a parlor and sit down?"

"Yes, of course," Lady Fairchild said in the same distant voice. "Damford, will you arrange for some hot tea to be sent in?"

"Of course, milady."

With an equanimity most of her pupils would have envied, Mrs. Merriweather followed Lady Fairchild into a room a short way down the hall. It was done in cheerful tones of yellow and blue. Not precisely to the former governess's taste, but just what she would have imagined Anna might choose.

She was right. "This is my favorite room," Lady Fairchild said quietly as she gestured for the other woman to be seated. "Edward let me have it papered and furnished just as I wished. No one will bother us here."

Mrs. Merriweather nodded, even as she pulled off her gloves and set them in her lap. "Good. Still, you had best tell me what is wrong at once. It is always a mistake to presume that no one will intrude."

"Wrong?" Lady Fairchild echoed with a short, high, nervous laugh.

Mrs. Merriweather sighed. "Do not waste my time, Anna. I know you far too well for this nonsense. It was evident from your letter that something is wrong and that was why you asked for me to come and visit you. Well, I am here. So tell me what is wrong and I will do my best to help you see your way clear of it."

When Lady Fairchild still hesitated, Mrs. Merriweather snapped, "Well? What is it? An affair? Have you been unfaithful and Lord Fairchild discovered it?"

"No!"

There was no mistaking Lady Fairchild's appalled shock at the question. The former governess bit back a smile. "Very well, then, unless you wish me to put my imagination to even more lurid thoughts, I suggest you simply screw up your courage and tell me what is wrong."

It was Lady Fairchild's turn to sigh. She rose to her feet and took a turn about the room before she answered. Finally she came and sat directly across from Mrs. Merriweather.

"You are right, of course. At least, I think you are. I could tell you that I wished for advice in seeking to replace my daughter's governess and it would be the truth. But it is more than that. I don't know if there is a problem or, if there is, how grave it might be. I only know that I am very much afraid that Lord Fairchild is keeping secrets from me and that is why I asked you here."

As Mrs. Merriweather and Lady Fairchild conversed in the blue and yellow parlor, the Countess of Kendall was showing Lady Winley and her daughter to their rooms. Since they possessed a certain number of acquaintances in common, Lady Winley and Lady Kendall were soon on excellent terms. Pamela Fairchild and Catherine Winley were sent off to, as the older ladies put it, amuse themselves. They, therefore, found themselves free to talk.

"I am glad you could come," Pamela said with a marked restraint as they walked toward the portrait gallery.

Catherine smiled and Pamela's heart sank. Miss Winley was indeed as beautiful as Julian had said. Her own efforts to redeem her appearance with a modish dress of blue muslin and her hair newly cut seemed ridiculous by comparison. Nor did it improve her mood to discover that Miss Winley was also as good-natured. Now the other girl looked at Pamela. There was diffidence in her tone as she replied, "I am very grateful to you for this invitation. I know that Mr. Deerwood said you would be kind enough to extend it, but I was certain he must be mistaken. And I had a particular reason for wishing to come to Kendall Hall."

"Yes, I know."

Miss Winley looked at Pamela oddly, as though she wished to say more, but she did not. Pamela could not help but feel grateful. To be forced to endure a listing of all Julian's admirable qualities could not help but hurt, if it came from Miss Winley.

As though she sensed something of Pamela's mood, Catherine linked her arm through that of her hostess and said, "I am certain we shall be good friends! Mr. Deerwood has told me so much about you that I feel as if I know you already."

That, of course, went some distance toward mollifying Pamela's spirits. She chided herself for foolish jealousy and set herself to entertain her guest. In a short time they made their way out to the gardens and that was where Julian found them.

Julian's first sight of Pamela and Catherine together brought a profound shock. Was this truly his childhood companion? He could not ever recall seeing her in anything other than an old gown as she sat by his side fishing or scampered through the woods with him. Was this the girl who said she cared nothing for her appearance? The girl he had called plain?

For she wasn't plain. Not dressed in a new and fashionable gown of pale blue muslin, her hair cropped and curled, her eyes sparkling with mischief at something Miss Winley had said.

Miss Winley! Abruptly Julian realized that his thoughts ought to be on her. He hastily stepped forward to greet her. Both ladies noticed him at the same moment.

As for Pamela, had she seen the way Julian looked at her the moment before, it might have brightened her spirits. But she only saw how resolutely he made his way straight for Miss Winley.

His manners were as impeccable as if they were in the drawing room under the watchful eye of Lady Winley. Which, perhaps, they were. Pamela thought she saw someone watching them out of an upstairs window and perhaps Julian was conscious of the scrutiny as well for he made no effort to touch Miss Winley. He did not try to take her hand or even gaze at her longingly, as Pamela supposed he must wish to do.

And yet there was that in his eyes that could not help but cause her distress. Was she a fool for inviting Miss Winley as Julian had asked? She had hoped that upon close inspection he would see it was nothing more than a passing fancy. Now she feared it was not.

Pamela had hoped, moreover, that Julian would value her good nature in doing this favor for him. That was what her mother, Lady Fairchild, would have said. But he only seemed to take her kindness as his due. Mama, Pamela thought gloomily, was often wrong.

Still, Julian was her friend. She cared for him and wished him to be happy. Truly she did. And if his happiness meant that he would become betrothed to Miss Winley, well, then Pamela would just have to find a way to be happy for him. And if her own heart was breaking, she was far too wise to think that love could be forced upon anyone else.

". . . do you think, Miss Fairchild?"

Abruptly Pamela realized that both Julian and Miss Winley were looking at her with an expectant air. "Forgive me, I was woolgathering. What did you say?"

"I was telling Miss Winley that surely your mother could have no objection to a ball being held at Kendall Hall," Julian said with an innocent air that fooled none of them.

"You would like a ball, wouldn't you?" Miss Winley

added her appeal. "I have not seen you in London yet and surely you would like to have the chance to dance?"

Pamela forbore from saying that she danced quite often enough, thank you. For one thing, she did not think the country dances hereabouts would impress Miss Winley. For another, she had a strong dislike of lying and it was true she did long for the day she would be able to waltz at Almack's. Another year, her mother said, having a strong dislike and disapproval of launching a girl too young.

Suddenly Pamela made up her mind. "I shall ask my mother directly. For you are right, I should like it above all things. Whether my mother will agree or not is another question. I am not yet out, you see."

"Yes, but tell her you wish it for the entertainment of your guest and so that you may acquire a comfort on the dance floor before you are exposed to the censorious eyes in London," Julian urged.

Pamela looked at him and grinned. "You have always known how to turn my mother up sweet, haven't you? Perhaps you'd best come along and have your touch at it, too."

So it was a party of three that trooped back into the house and looked for Lady Fairchild. They found her with an odd dab of a woman who despite her diminutive stature seemed almost to radiate authority. Miss Winley recognized her at once.

"Oh, dear," she murmured. "I fear Mama gave that woman a severe setdown on the front steps. Perhaps I should leave this to the two of you, after all."

But it was too late. All three had been seen and had to come forward and be introduced to Mrs. Merriweather. When Lady Fairchild pronounced her daughter's name, Mrs. Merriweather had the oddest reaction. She seemed to start choking, and were she not a stranger to them all, Pamela would have thought the woman on the verge of laughing. Her words seemed to reinforce that notion.

She looked at Lady Fairchild and said, "I should have known. Novels were ever your weakness."

For the first time in her life, Pamela saw her mother at a loss for words. It was such an unsettling notion that she made haste to divert this strange woman's attention.

"We have a scheme, Mr. Deerwood and Miss Winley and I, and you must give us your opinion of it, Mrs. Merriweather. We think it would be the nicest thing if Mama were to hold a ball while Miss Winley is visiting."

Again an odd look passed between the two older women. Lady Fairchild drew herself upright in her chair. "Pamela is not yet out and I cannot think it wise to subject her to the sort of gossip that would occur were she seen to be dancing at a formal ball here at Kendall Hall," she said.

"Oh, not a formal ball," Miss Winley blurted out. "A masquerade. Then no one need know how much she dances. Particularly if she retires before the unmasking."

Pamela gaped at the young woman. Even Julian seemed taken aback. Lady Fairchild looked as if she meant to give the girl a setdown. It was, oddly enough, Mrs. Merriweather who decided the matter. In a remarkably gentle voice and with a wistful smile upon her face she said, "You know, Anna, you were always fond of balls. And masquerades. Particularly masquerades. I remember one—"

"Yes, yes," Lady Fairchild said hastily. "I recollect the one quite clearly, thank you, Miss Tibbles!"

The young people looked at one another askance and Lady Fairchild became even more flustered. "That is to say, thank you, Mrs. Merriweather. I forget, sometimes, that you have married since I knew you."

"I, on the other hand," Mrs. Merriweather said

dryly, "have forgotten nothing. And I think it would indeed be a shame to deny the young people their pleasure. Unless, of course, you have another reason for wishing to say no? But I have always found that a little innocent pleasure goes a long way to averting disastrous ones."

Lady Fairchild looked much struck by these words and, a moment or two later, gave her consent. "Yes, very well, we shall hold a masquerade. In a week's time, I think. That will allow us to send out invitations and make all the arrangements. Pamela, I shall expect your help in this!"

"Of course, Mama," Pamela replied in a demure voice.

"Very well, now you had best all be off. I've no doubt you wish to plan your costumes and I wish to continue my comfortable coze with Miss Tibbles. I mean, Mrs. Merriweather."

No one had any real objection to this plan.

Chapter 4

One week. Not much time. And none of the household rested easy. There was too much to do, too much fussing over the cost, too much whispering in dark corners of Kendall Hall. The only ones who appeared oblivious to all of this unease were the young people. But they had troubles of their own.

They were in the garden, Pamela and Julian. She was, as usual, listening to his concerns and wondering whether she should share with him her own.

"Miss Winley is all that is sweet and agreeable," Julian complained, "except when I try to talk to her about how I feel. Then she will hear none of it."

"Perhaps," Pamela said doubtfully, "she is merely a very properly brought up young lady? Mama is forever telling me I must not show any encouragement to any man until Papa has consented to letting the man court me."

Julian made a dismissive gesture with his hand. "Catherine would think nothing of that," he scoffed, "if her heart were truly engaged."

Since Pamela was inclined to agree with this assessment, she could think of nothing reassuring to say. Finally she ventured a question about the masquerade.

"Have you chosen your costume yet?" she asked.

He kicked at a stone near his foot and thrust his hands into his pockets. "How can I," he demanded, "when Miss Winley refuses to tell me what she will wear?"

Now it was Pamela who made a sound of disgust. "For heaven's sake, Julian! Wear anything. You will still look handsome and she will see how very agreeable a partner you may be."

"Do you think so? But I should so like for us to have been a matched pair."

Pamela made another exclamation of disgust. Then she said, with pardonable exasperation, "As well shout to the world your intentions toward Miss Winley!"

"So? Why should I not?"

"Because Lady Winley would have her daughter bundled up and out of here before the final chords of music died," Pamela retorted. "You cannot have mistaken how little she favors your suit. She is already suspicious since she discovered how young my brothers are. Were it not for this masquerade ball, I think Lady Winley would already have packed her bags and left. I think Miss Winley shows great wisdom in refusing to tell you what she means to wear. If you wish to continue to be able to see her here, you'd best take your lead from her. She, at least, shows admirable discretion."

"I don't wish to be discreet," Julian grumbled.

But Pamela knew her childhood friend well enough to be able to guess that she had given him a great deal to think about and that he would. So she turned the talk to other, lighter matters. Such as how his favorite hunting dog was doing and whether he was satisfied with his new rifle. It was only as he was leaving that Julian seemed to realize something was amiss.

He paused and looked at her more carefully. "Is something troubling you, Pamela?"

She did not at once answer and he took her hands in his. Then she looked up at him. "I am not entirely certain," she said. "Mama says that everything is all right, but I see her watching Papa with worried eyes. And even my grandfather seems lost in thought these days. But perhaps I am simply being foolish."

"Perhaps. But I should rather you told me than tried to bear these worries yourself," Julian scolded sternly.

She smiled a trifle wistfully at him. "You have had other matters on your mind."

He winced at that, knowing it to be true that he had thought about little save Miss Winley these past few days. So now he tried to make amends.

"I always have time for you," he said. "And for your worries. We have always helped one another and I do not mean to stop now."

"How sweet!" a voice said from behind them.

Julian and Pamela turned to find Miss Winley regarding them with a sardonic expression that was almost a sneer. She took a step forward toward them.

"You profess to adore me, Mr. Deerwood," Catherine Winley said, looking from one to the other, "but I find you holding hands with Miss Fairchild?"

Julian started to drop the hand he was still holding, but abruptly gripped it even tighter. He tilted up his chin and his voice was level as he said, "Miss Fairchild and I have been friends most of our lives. I do not abandon my friends for anyone."

Miss Winley gave a trill of laughter. "Abandon her? Miss Fairchild scarcely is abandoned when surrounded by her family. Nor should I call her precisely helpless. Pray do not lie to me and call your affection for her anything other than what it is. I am not a fool."

These last words were spoken rather sharply and Julian was more taken aback than ever. There was no trace of the good-natured young lady he had come to know in the termagant who stood before them now. He met malice with cold civility.

"Nor am I a fool," he said.

It was left to Pamela to be the diplomat. "As I am the cause of this quarrel, I shall remove myself at once. The two of you may settle this as you will. You might recollect, however, Miss Winley, that if I stood upon such terms with Mr. Deerwood as you imagine, it would have been most unlikely that I would have invited you here as my guest."

And then, head held high, Pamela walked away. Behind her she could hear the murmur of voices, and the moment she was out of sight of Julian and Catherine, she took to her heels and ran the rest of the way to the house. She did not care that anyone watching would think her indecorous. Her goal was to reach the safety of her room before anyone could catch her as she started to cry. Let Julian and Catherine fight as they wished. It was none of her affair, after all.

All she wished to do, Pamela thought crossly, was to forget the quickness with which Julian had denied the possibility that he felt more for her than the simple brotherly affection of an old childhood friend. It was a truth she knew only too well and she did not see why she need be reminded of it at every turn.

Mrs. Merriweather was facing a crisis of her own. She stood in the hallway outside the nursery and stared at the woman before her.

"What did you say?" she asked incredulously.

The nurse's voice was properly deferential but implacable. "I've put the children down for a nap and you'll have to come back later."

"But I wish to see my daughter. This is the hour I always read to her," Mrs. Merriweather protested.

The woman crossed her arms. "Not in this house. I'll not have the children's schedule upset by every guest who comes to stay. It's not good for them."

Was that a sniff of disdain? Mrs. Merriweather's eyes narrowed. She visibly bristled. "My good woman, do you know who I am?" she asked softly in a voice that had intimidated dukes and earls and countesses over the years.

Definitely a sniff of disdain. "I don't know and I don't care. I told Lady Kendall, when I was hired on years ago, that if she wanted my services, then I would have a free hand in the nursery. And I do. And I say the children nap now."

"We shall see about that!"

Marian took a step forward. The nurse physically blocked her way. She started to speak. She stopped. She took the measure of the woman before her, turned on her heel, and stormed away.

Over her shoulder, Mrs. Merriweather called back in a cold voice, "Lady Fairchild shall hear about this outrage at once!"

Unfortunately, she found Anna somewhat less than sympathetic. Instead of being properly indignant, the woman started to laugh!

"I am so sorry, Miss Tibbles, but you must see how amusing it is. Why, when I think of the manner in which you dared to order my parents about, I can only think this is fair turnabout for you!"

Mrs. Merriweather would have retreated then, but Lady Fairchild held out a hand to forestall her. "Wait," she said. "I am truly sorry and I shall speak to the nursery staff. But please, I need your advice."

Advice? That was different. Mrs. Merriweather sat down again. "Of course, my dear. How can I help?"

Lady Fairchild twisted her handkerchief in her hands. "It is this ball I am giving for the young people."

"Surely you are accustomed to such things by now?"

"Yes, but I am not certain I should have agreed, you see. The expense. And Pamela is so young."

"Not too young to need to acquire a bit of experience in such situations," Marian said dryly. "It is my opinion, as you well know, that casting a girl into the *ton* without the chance to practice her manners, in a milieu such as this, is a grave error."

"Yes, yes, I know. It is just that every time I think

of this ball, I have the most horrid feeling. And Lord
Fairchild won't speak of it at all!"

Mrs. Merriweather hesitated. She did not dismiss
such words out of hand. She did not call them foolish
nonsense. Anna was not a rattlepate, though there
were times her parents had thought her one. Nor was
she subject to megrims. Not back then, at any rate.
Had she changed?

The former governess studied her former charge
closely. No, Anna was much the same as she had always been. Therefore, Mrs. Merriweather considered
the words, the fears, with the gravity they deserved.
And though Anna could not explain any of it, both
women were a great deal graver after their talk than
before.

Catherine Winley stared out of the window, her re-
cent quarrel with Deerwood fresh in her mind. The
quarrel she had fled, seeking refuge at her mother's
side. She had been foolish to roast him as she did.
But how was she to know he would become so cross?
Or that Miss Fairchild would be so offended. Would
she try to send her away?

But Catherine would not have taken back the
words, even if she could. Mr. Deerwood presumed too
much upon their short acquaintance. That he did so
upon encouragement from her, that she had given him
sufficient cause to believe he had a right to do so, was
more than she cared to acknowledge. And yet fear
made her head ache.

Had she made a mistake to come? No. An image
formed in her mind of the handsome man she cared
for. She had to see him again. Talk to him. And she
would. On the night of the ball she would tell him
precisely what she wished of him. She could only pray
he felt the same.

Behind her daughter, Lady Winley sat glancing
through the latest issue of *La Belle Assemblée*. "This

would be a most flattering dress for you, Catherine,"
she said thoughtfully. "Of course one would have to
alter the bodice a trifle. And I do not think large
fabric flowers all over the dress would be flattering to
you. Or to anyone. But in other respects it is just what
one would like."

Dutifully Catherine came over to peruse the picture.
She pronounced it acceptable and managed to deflect
her mother's shrewd gaze by pointing to another print
and saying she would like to have a riding habit made
up in just such a style.

"No, no, no! You cannot mean it, surely?" Lady
Winley protested in shocked accents. "It would not
flatter you in the least. And you would be pronounced
a brazen hussy were you to attempt the style."

"But Mama," Catherine said with an ingenuous,
wide-eyed stare, "if it is so exceptionable, why is it in
La Belle Assemblée?"

Flustered, Lady Winley could only reply, "Because
it is intended for a married woman. A rather dashing
married woman. Not a young girl. Depend upon it, if
you wore such a creation, you would be declared fast."

"Yes, Mama. How fortunate I am to have you to
guide me."

Lady Winley paused, her intended scold cut short
by such penitence. Her expression faltered and then
she smiled as her thoughts took on new direction.

"Well, yes, I do think," she said cautiously, "that
you are fortunate. I flatter myself to think there are
few who understand the dictates of society as well as
I do."

"Oh, I am certain of it, Mama!"

Before Lady Winley could long indulge the unwelcome suspicion that her daughter was making game
of her, the door to the small parlor opened and a
young man poked in his head. She was not pleased to
see that it was that young man from the neighborhood

making free with Kendall Hall in a way that was most reprehensible. His expression was grim.

"Ah, there you are! We did not, I think, finish our conversation."

"Mr. Deerwood!" Catherine said, with patent constraint. "Come in. And do, I beg you, greet my mama as well."

The young man blanched at the sight of Lady Winley. A most disturbing sign, the older woman thought. Majestically she greeted him, doing everything in her power to intimidate the boy.

"Mr. Deerwood? You are no doubt looking for Miss Fairchild. I believe her to be in the gardens."

But he was not so easily routed as she expected and Lady Winley began to feel a reluctant respect for the boy. It still would not do, of course, but she could not deny there was a great deal of character in the way he faced her squarely, meeting her eyes without hesitation. And in the way he answered her attempt to divert him.

"Miss Fairchild and I were concerned about Miss Winley. She did not seem quite herself a little while ago. I thought perhaps she might like to come outside and reassure Miss Fairchild, herself."

Lady Winley could not help but notice that Catherine had gone pale and retreated a step or two. So they had had a falling-out, had the two? Excellent! Though she did not like Mr. Deerwood's impertinence in following her daughter to this room to continue the quarrel.

Abruptly Lady Winley changed her mind and did not give Deerwood the setdown. It would be better, she thought, if it came from her daughter so instead she turned to and said, "Catherine?"

"I, er, that is, no, I should prefer to stay indoors this morning. I seem to, er, have taken a chill."

"A chill? We must do something! Can I get you anything?" her mother said at once.

Deerwood merely looked grimmer than before. His voice was unyielding as he said, "Then of course you must stay here. I shall make your apologies to Miss Fairchild. No doubt she will wish to come and see what she can do for you."

That seemed to alarm Catherine even more. "No! I pray you, I shall be fine. Please tell Miss Fairchild she need not worry about me at all."

Deerwood bowed and withdrew. The moment he was gone, Lady Winley pursed her lips together in a thin smile.

"That was well done, Catherine. Well done indeed. It would not do to encourage such a paltry fellow as that. Not when we have an earl and a marquis almost come up to scratch. I am most pleased to see that you comprehend the situation as clearly as do I."

If Catherine's reply was a somewhat colorless "Yes, Mama," at least it was not disagreement, and with that, Lady Winley was perfectly willing to be content.

Chapter 5

The day of the ball arrived overcast but by mid-afternoon had cleared, a circumstance that pleased almost everyone at Kendall Hall and indeed much of the surrounding countryside.

Only Lord Fairchild grew graver as the day wore on. He withdrew to the study, saying he had no patience for such nonsense as was going on all about the place. When Lady Fairchild would have joined him, he refused her company with a curt word and the shake of his head.

Mrs. Merriweather watched this byplay with a sinking heart. Anna had always been a favorite of hers. To be sure, perhaps every governess felt that way about her first charge, but it was more than that. In many ways she had identified with Anna more than any other of her charges and she truly wished to see Anna happy. And at the moment Lady Fairchild was not.

For various reasons, therefore, the day seemed to drag for every member of the household. But at last it was time to don the finery, time to line up to greet the guests.

Pamela might have been pardoned for taking pride in how she looked. A Grecian gown of white silk showed her figure off to advantage and there was a glow about her face and eyes that could not help but please. Indeed, the look upon Mr. Deerwood's face when he saw her sufficed to assure her that the time and care she had taken in choosing her costume had not been wasted.

He was dressed as the handsome woodsman Robin Hood for, as he had confided to Pamela earlier, he thought Miss Winley might well choose to be Maid Marian. She was grateful that she had both resisted the temptation to tell him Miss Winley had another costume in mind entirely and the temptation to dress as Maid Marian herself. For as it was, he bent over her hand, stammered out a compliment to her looks, and moved on, dazed, to where her mother and father stood dressed as members of the Renaissance Italian DeMedici family. Pamela's grandparents had chosen Italian costumes as well. Lord Kendall happily proclaimed himself as Machiavelli while Lady Kendall refused to discuss the matter at all. Lady Gwendolyn and her children were dressed as members of King Arthur's court and Richard even wore a sword of sorts at his side.

Miss Winley and her mother came downstairs to the ballroom after the first guests had already arrived. Apparently the arranging of fairy wings was a trifle more complicated than anticipated. And Julian's dismay at the disarrangement of his plans regarding their costumes made him ill equipped to judge how well Miss Winley's costume suited her.

Soon it was time to dance. Julian Deerwood could not lead out Miss Winley, however much he may have wished to do so. That honor belonged to Pamela's cousin, Richard Avery. And he did so with a charming smile and a degree of town bronze that Julian could not hope to match.

Indeed, Julian discovered a hitherto unsuspected streak of violence in his breast as he contemplated various ways he might dispatch the young man he had always, up to this point at any rate, admired. His partner, Pamela, smiled consolingly.

"Never mind," she said. "You shall have your

chance to dance with her later. And this will throw dust in Lady Winley's eyes."

"And in mine," Julian could not help but reply.

Pamela snorted. "Nonsense! If Miss Winley cares for you, one dance with Richard will not alter her affections. Now come, at least present an appearance of complacence, if you please, with my company."

At that, Julian looked at his childhood friend, really looked at her, and immediately felt a pang of regret. "I am sorry, Pamela. I've no right to treat you in such a way. You deserve far better."

From that moment on until he left her company to ask another young lady to dance, Julian gave Pamela his full attention and even managed to make her laugh a time or two. And if, when he left her side, he made his way to Miss Winley's, well, Pamela would not allow it to signify.

One of the brief times she was alone, without a partner, her father joined her. "Enjoying the ball?" he asked.

Pamela smiled. "Of course, Father. How could I not?"

He touched her arm then pointed to Julian. "Perhaps you would rather be dancing with him than watching him dance with someone else, eh?" And then he stroked her arm as he said, "You should be dancing yourself. Care to take a turn about the room with me?"

"But they are waltzing, Papa! I cannot do so before I am even out. People will say I am fast!"

"Oh, come, they cannot say so if you are dancing with your father," he protested.

Perhaps he was right. Perhaps there was nothing to trouble her in the suggestion, but nonetheless Pamela was troubled. There was also an odd edge to her father's voice that became more pronounced with everything he said.

But there was no way to refuse. Before she knew

it, he had drawn her onto the dance floor. She had no
choice but to waltz or to create a spectacle that would
have been even worse. Neither of them could have
liked that.

Papa must, she decided, just want to make certain
that she did not sit out even one dance. Certainly he
relinquished her to another young gentleman from the
neighborhood with the greatest good humor the moment the waltz ended. In any event, the joy of taking
part in her first masquerade ball soon displaced all
thoughts of someone so mundane as a father.

Mrs. Merriweather observed the ball with great interest. She had always enjoyed watching people and
she found them most entertaining in circumstances
such as this. She liked to see young people enjoy
themselves, the opinions of some of her former
charges to the contrary. She liked to see older people
enjoy themselves as well. Nor was she averse to taking
a turn or two about the floor in the company of a
handsome gentleman herself. She did not think Colonel Merriweather would mind. Indeed, she could almost hear his voice telling her: "For heaven's sake,
enjoy yourself, Marian!"

So she did. She even had the satisfaction of twirling
about the floor with one of them when the musicians
struck up a waltz. It was poorly done, of course, when
the daughter of the house, Miss Fairchild, could not
be permitted to enjoy the dance. Except that she was
waltzing! Had Anna taught her daughter nothing?

But then Mrs. Merriweather realized that the girl
was dancing with her father. Perhaps that made it all
right, but it was not something she would have recom-
mended had she had the schooling of the girl. Still,
she thought, it was not her affair. And she could well
understand the temptation. Indeed, she suspected
more than one young gentleman had bribed the musi-

cians to play the waltz so that they could dance it with the young lady they liked best.

It was at the end of this lively exercise that Mrs. Merriweather retreated to what she hoped would be a quiet nook in which to catch her breath. Here, unseen, she could still observe some of the sights of the ball and hear the strains of music. Too late she realized she could hear far more than that.

Couples walked past her, men and women deep in conversation. Voices carried to where she sat. Most of the conversations were not in the least interesting and she paid them no mind. But the same voice kept intruding over and over again. And every time, no matter who the fellow was talking with, the other person was upset. Understandably so, for this fellow seemed to talk only in anger, only in threats. Marian began to grow quite impatient with the fellow. Must he cause such trouble on an occasion such as this?

Finally, unable to bear it no longer, she leaned out of the nook to see if she could see who the troublemaker was. She suffered a severe setback when she did for the fellow, despite his costume, was unmistakably Lord Fairchild.

Hastily Mrs. Merriweather leaned back so that he would not see her. To say that she was shocked was a decided understatement. For she had heretofore considered Anna's husband to be a harmless if not terribly cordial host. He had seemed neither rude nor inviting. He could be counted upon to ignore everyone equally. So to discover him now engaged in conversation with several people, all upon menacing terms, was a decided shock.

It greatly lowered her opinion of the man and gave Mrs. Merriweather her first glimpse into the reason Anna was so unhappy. It was not the first time that she had encountered a gentleman who presented one face to guests and another to intimates. But it was the first time she had thought that Lord Fairchild might be such a one.

It was a most lowering reflection to realize that her mental acuity appeared to be diminishing. For it was the one thing she had been able to count upon her entire life. Perhaps it was this depressing thought that caused her not to see or overhear at least one of the encounters this gentleman had with the guests at Kendall Hall.

Mrs. Merriweather did pause to wonder who the guests were Lord Fairchild had been browbeating in such a way, but each of them had taken far greater pains to conceal their identities than had his lordship. And since they might well have been strangers to her anyway, her curiosity went unsatisfied.

Still, it had never been her nature to repine overmuch upon the evil of the world. So, after allowing herself a few moments of melancholy reflection, Mrs. Merriweather shook off her megrims and returned to the dance floor. There was a major who had requested the pleasure of a dance. And since he had once known Colonel Merriweather, she did not wish to disappoint the gentleman.

It was, after all, such a delight whenever she could collect anecdotes about the colonel from such fellows, stories that were warranted to embarrass him when next she revealed to him what she had discovered. From the way the fellow's eyes had twinkled when he mentioned the colonel, Mrs. Merriweather thought that this would be just such a satisfying, and productive, occasion.

It was at the end of this dance that she had her own encounter with Lord Fairchild. She found him waiting to solicit her hand for a dance. And how could she refuse? Besides, this was her chance to probe how matters stood between him and Anna. So she accepted and they took their place in the country dance. For several moments he seemed content merely to move through the figures of the dance.

But then he smiled at her in a most disturbing way and said, "No doubt you will think me foolish, but I should like to tell you I think you far more beautiful than half the young creatures here."

Mrs. Merriweather almost missed a step, so unexpected was the compliment. She could think of nothing to answer, but it did not seem that Lord Fairchild expected an answer. He merely smiled as they were separated by the dance and, when they came together again, perfectly ready to carry the conversation himself.

"You have changed since you were Anna's governess."

By now she had found her tongue. "Most of us have, over the years," she replied tartly.

He conceded the point with a nod of his head. "Tell me what you think of Anna, as she is now."

But this was too much. Mrs. Merriweather shook her head. "I should not presume to do so."

"Oh, come! It is strictly between us. I should be curious to know what you think."

Clearly he meant to persist until she answered him. Forgetting that he was her host and the son of an earl, Mrs. Merriweather drew herself up straighter and said sharply, "I find Anna to have grown into a remarkably handsome and sensible woman."

He nodded. "Very diplomatically spoken. And does she seem happy?"

"Surely you can tell me that better than I could presume to tell you?"

"Ah, but I am curious as to your opinion. And your opinion of Pamela."

Here at least Mrs. Merriweather could speak to the point. "I like Pamela very much! She is a very pretty girl and, more importantly, a well-mannered one with what I judge to be a kind and gentle nature. You have done well by her."

Something glittered in Lord Fairchild's eyes then, something Mrs. Merriweather found most disturbing though she could not have said what it was. She was most profoundly grateful that a moment later the music came to an end and she could plead the need to sit down. With relief she saw that a neighborhood matron was bearing down upon them with a patent desire for speech with Lord Fairchild. Mrs. Merriweather grasped the opportunity to make good her escape.

Catherine Winley slipped down the hallway. There was no one about and perhaps now she would have a chance to meet privately with her swain. There had not been one such moment since the ball began and it was imperative she speak with him alone.

She would have been appalled had she known who saw and followed her.

It was sometime later that Daphne Avery slipped back into the ballroom. Had anyone noticed her absence? Had she sufficiently repaired the damage to her dress? She was delighted to discover that no one seemed to pay her the slightest attention.

One might have thought that a still attractive, albeit single, woman of three-and-thirty would wish for attention, but it was otherwise with Daphne. Tonight she devoutly prayed that no one would notice her. That no one would notice the way her hands trembled or the repairs to her gown. She prayed that no one would ask where she had been or what she had done. For she could not have answered. Only her brother, Richard, saw her and would have come to her side but stopped when she shook her head, warning him away.

She had thought herself safe. And now, in just a few horrible moments, the terror had all come flooding back again. This time she had escaped, but would she next? Almost she changed her mind about telling Richard. He would stand by her, no matter what. That much Daphne knew. But in the end she said nothing. She could not imagine doing so without losing her composure entirely and that would draw precisely the attention she most wished to avoid.

Lady Kendall watched her niece slip back into the ballroom and sighed. It was a pity Daphne had never married. But she had been adamant, turning down every suitor who had offered for her hand. At one time Lady Kendall had feared the girl had a *tendre* for Harry, but she had apparently been mistaken in that. Which was fortunate for the connection was too close for her to be pleased with a match between the cousins.

Still, she wondered and worried about Daphne and her brother, Richard. Both should long since have left Kendall Hall and found a life elsewhere. Of course, Mr. Avery had left his wife and offspring without any support and indeed with an insurmountable wall of debts so that Lord Kendall had had no choice but to offer his sister a place in his home. It had been a necessary but scarcely, in Lady Kendall's opinion, felicitous arrangement.

Lady Kendall looked about for her son, Lord Fairchild, and frowned. She did not like the way he was moving about the room and laughing. Nor the way his wife, Anna, carefully averted her eyes whenever he looked her way but then watched him with unguarded longing when he did not. There was a problem there and one that had best be rectified as soon as might be. Her efforts to talk with Edward had been futile. He would tell her and his father nothing.

For a moment she thought she saw something in the way he moved, the way others responded to him, that reminded her of another. Her hand crept to her

throat and she chided herself for her foo...
Harry was dead, long dead, and it was only her ima...
nation that caused her to see more resemblance than
there truly was. That was the problem with having
twins. They mirrored each other in ways that went
beyond mere appearance.

The countess spared scarcely a glance for the
houseguests. Odd enough that her granddaughter had
invited a girl she did not know to come and visit, for
that was patently the case, whatever nonsense Pamela
tried to claim to anyone else. Nor would she allow
any thoughts to be wasted on the woman who had
been a governess. Really, it was the outside of enough
for Anna to have invited the creature, but given that
she felt the need, the woman ought to have had sense
enough to keep to her room during festivities such as
this instead of making a cake of herself by dancing!
Even her marriage to some colonel or other could not
wipe out the reality of who she had been, what she
had spent most of her life doing.

Finally Lady Kendall looked about for her husband,
the Earl of Kendall. She frowned when she could not
find him. Was he feeling tired again? Needing to rest?
It worried her that he seemed so much older these
days. Their marriage might have begun, as so many
did, as a sensible affair arranged between their parents, but she and Kendall had come to feel a strong
degree of affection for each other and now, as they
grew older together, she worried about him more than
he might have liked.

Tapping her chin thoughtfully with the fan she carried, Lady Kendall began making her way unobtru-
sively toward the door of the ballroom. If her husband
were feeling unwell, she really ought to check on him.

The Earl of Kendall, however, did not want to be
found. He stood half hidden by draperies as he
watched the ball. What he saw disturbed him greatly.
Like his wife, he worried about Lord and Lady Fair-

...ied about Richard and Daphne.
...e worried about Pamela. He knew
...have favorites, but he did. Perhaps it
...it, of all his children and grandchildren
...id nephews, Pamela was the one who
r... ...m most of himself.

He... watched her dance and more than once felt
a desire to stride from his hiding place and plant a
facer on some gentleman's complacent countenance.
But he did not. No, for the moment he would watch
and wait. And tomorrow he would talk with Pamela.
He had the notion something was troubling her. But
whether it was the trouble between her parents, or
the way that young puppy, Julian Deerwood, mooned
over Miss Winley, or something else entirely, he did
not yet know.

Lady Gwendolyn also watched the dancers. She sat
surrounded by friends and yet she could not feel other
than a pang of grief for lost opportunities as she
watched the couples move about the floor. Daphne
should by now be married and providing her with
grandchildren to fuss over. Richard should be a leader
of the *ton*. And she, she should have her own compe-
tence, rather than being dependent upon the charity
of her brother.

But it was not so and not likely ever to be so. She
sighed then hastily smiled. It would not do for anyone
to know how discontented she was in her state. For
that had never been her way. She would make the
best of things, as she always had.

Still, it was difficult to watch her niece, Pamela, and
know that the girl had her future before her. It might
be a wonderful one and clearly the girl thought so.
But it was also possible it would be as lonely, as disap-
pointing as her own had been. And Lady Gwendolyn
found that she could not wish such a fate on anyone.
Not even Pamela.

Chapter 6

The ball ended well after midnight and only the presence of a full moon allowed the various parties to depart with some sense of comfort. Then the guests and family members resident at Kendall Hall made their way upstairs to their various rooms. Lady Fairchild and Lady Kendall and Lady Gwendolyn and Lady Winley and Mrs. Merriweather all kept a sharp eye out to make certain that no one mistook their room and everyone ended up where they ought to be.

"For after an evening such as this where the wine flows freely, there is no knowing what sorts of mistakes a gentleman may make," Lady Kendall pronounced austerely.

The other ladies all nodded, understanding quite perfectly what she meant. And none of them wishing to risk that any young lady might make such a mistake either.

It was therefore perhaps not surprising that everyone was rather tired the next day and seemed a trifle confused. It began at breakfast. No one seemed very much inclined to talk. Only Lord Fairchild was in an affable mood. At least he was before he began.

"So, did everyone enjoy the ball?" he asked.

They stared at him, affronted. "It was a very nice ball," Mrs. Merriweather said, in her placid way. "Though I do think, Lord Fairchild, it was a mistake for you to waltz with Pamela. Even if you are her father, it might seem fast to others."

He gaped at her. "I? Waltz with Pamela?"

Now it was Pamela's turn to look bewildered. "Yes, Papa. You said it was unexceptionable because you are my father. But I did wonder if it were wise."

He went very pale, so pale that Lady Fairchild rose from her seat and would have gone to him. He waved her away. "No, no, it had simply slipped my mind," he said, with a very weak smile.

The others nodded politely, then looked away as though embarrassed for him. All, that is, save Mrs. Merriweather. She saw him look to his father, the Earl of Kendall, and exchange a worried look with him. And the countess had the strangest expression on her own face. Something very odd, indeed, was going on here. It was patent that Anna had no notion what it might be for she looked more bewildered than anyone else present.

Indeed, looking about the table, Marian realized that everyone seemed ill at ease, but most did not look confused. They looked, if anything, almost bitter.

Lady Winley regarded Fairchild with a pinched look about the eyes and mouth. "I think it most inappropriate," she said, "for a man of your years to dance with girls as young as Miss Fairchild or with my own daughter."

Fairchild's eyes widened and Daphne abruptly fled the breakfast parlor. Or she would have done so, in any event, if her mother had not grabbed the skirt of her dress and forced her to sit again.

It was the earl who distracted everyone. In a rather impatient voice he said, "This is the problem with balls and masquerades! Everyone is exhausted the next day and all but impossible to deal with. Add to that the fact that too many drink far too freely and both heads and memories are much the worse for it!"

He seemed merely irritable and Mrs. Merriweather might have believed it had he not then regarded each of them with eyes that seemed to study their reactions very closely. He seemed satisfied for he turned to his granddaughter and said, "Well, Pamela, will you join me for a game of chess? The board is already set up in my room."

"Of course, Grandfather," she said with a sweet smile.

Together they rose and quit the room. That seemed to be the signal others were waiting for and soon only Mrs. Merriweather and Lady Winley found themselves lingering over their breakfast, though Lady Winley watched her daughter go with worried eyes.

"Is something wrong?" Mrs. Merriweather asked gently when they were alone.

Lady Winley looked at her with disdain. "If there were, I should not tell you!"

"I know you dislike my company, but even you must allow I have more than a little experience dealing with young girls. If something is wrong, perhaps I can help."

It was a measure of Lady Winley's agitation that she set down her cup with a snap and said, a thread of indignation running through her words, "It is Catherine! She is oddly disturbed this morning. It may only be that Lord Fairchild displayed unexpected lecherous tendencies at the ball last night and she did not quite know how to counter them. But she will not tell me and I worry that it occupies her mind more than it ought."

"Would you like me to speak with her?" Mrs. Merriweather asked. "Sometimes a girl will speak with a stranger more easily than with her mother, particularly if she fears something she said or did provoked the behavior."

Lady Winley was patently torn. She did not wish to agree but her maternal concern overrode her dislike of Mrs. Merriweather, so in the end she nodded. "I should be grateful if you would," she said.

The former governess rose to her feet with her usual

calm manner. "I've a letter to write to my husband, but after that, I shall look for Catherine and see if I cannot put her fears to rest."

With the gravest reluctance, Lady Winley thanked her and both ladies parted, if not on terms of friendship, at least with a better opinion of each other than they each had had before.

The girl in question stood at the window of her room, a crumpled piece of paper in her hand and tears running down her cheeks. Who had seen them and how? She thought they had been most careful. Would the writer carry through on the threat? What could be done to prevent it?

The invitation to come for a stay here at Kendall Hall had seemed a gift from providence when it arrived. Now that same invitation seemed the most horrible curse. What on earth was she to do? Tell Mama they must leave? But to what point? The writer of this scurrilous note could as easily write to her in London as here. Or worse, what if the writer did not write but simply carried out the threat?

Money. The writer wanted money. But where would she obtain the sum mentioned? It was not as though her pin money would run to it. Nor could she ask her mother.

Catherine could see no way out and wondered what she was going to do if none appeared. She had heard all her life of girls being ruined by gossip and now it was she who faced that fate.

The Earl of Kendall regarded his granddaughter over the chessboard as she studied her next move. She looked up to see him watching her. A tiny frown creased her brow. "Is something wrong?" she asked. "Am I playing so poorly? Or are you tired?"

He shook his head. And made himself smile. "No,

of course not, my dear. I was just thinking about last night's masquerade ball."

Her expression faltered and her hand fell away from the piece she had been about to move. The earl cursed. "You are unhappy, aren't you?"

"No, of course not!"

The protest came immediately, instinctively. But the earl shook his head. "You may be honest with me, Pamela. I saw how you watched young Deerwood. And how he watched the Winley chit."

From a corner where Lady Kendall was doing her needlework there came a disapproving sound. "Pamela may look, indeed she ought to look, much higher for a husband than Deerwood. He is a nice enough young man, I will allow. But I will not, I cannot countenance, such a poor match for her. She is the granddaughter of an earl! Anna must take her to London and there she may marry as she ought. A viscount, at the very least, not a young man who will merely become a baron someday."

"And if she doesn't wish to marry a viscount?" the earl countered mildly.

Lady Kendall looked surprised. "What has that to say to anything? I did not want to marry you but I did my duty. And you cannot say that has turned out so badly, can you? This nonsense today about emotions and *tendres* is foolish beyond permission!"

The earl spied a glimpse of humor in his granddaughter's eyes as she bent her head forward and studied the board. Her voice sounded casual but he could see that her expression was not as she said, "Mama and Papa were subject to such foolishness, I believe."

"I've no doubt they were," Lady Kendall sniffed. "But had it not been an acceptable match, I should still not have agreed to it."

The earl started to speak then changed his mind. He continued to watch his granddaughter closely. After a moment he said, "I noticed that your father danced with you last night, Pamela. That was very kind of him for otherwise you could not have danced during the waltz."

She shivered. "Yes, yes, it was kind of him, I suppose."

"She should not have waltzed at all," Lady Kendall said, a harsh note in her voice.

"It was with her father," the earl reminded her.

"That does not matter! She should not have done so. Edward should have known better."

"He said he was certain it would be all right," Pamela said, an uncertain note in her voice.

The earl could see the troubled look in her eyes and she shivered again. "Is something wrong?" he asked.

But Pamela only shook her head. How could she tell them how odd Papa had seemed? Or the way he had held her or touched her arm in a way that did not seem in the least paternal. It must have been her imagination! Papa would never behave in such a way, after all.

But still the troubled look on her face, the discomfort inside, lingered and it could only be a relief when the game came to an end and she could flee the room. It didn't matter that she had lost; it didn't matter the excuse she found. She was away from her grandfather's shrewd regard and her grandmother's ambitions.

Mrs. Merriweather found Catherine Winley in the portrait gallery. The younger girl turned at the sound of footsteps, a smile on her face. It faded the moment she saw who was there.

"Oh, hullo, Mrs. Merriweather."

The former governess raised her eyebrows. "You look a trifle pale, Miss Winley."

"Oh, it is, it must be, lack of sleep. You must know I did not go to bed before dawn."

Mrs. Merriweather nodded and smiled the cynical

smile of a governess who has heard far better and more convincing explanations in her career. "And is that all, my dear?" she asked gently.

"W-what else could it be?" Miss Winley stammered.

"Your mother told me that Lord Fairchild was a trifle, er, more familiar than he ought to have been?"

"Oh, that."

Marian could have sworn there was relief in Miss Winley's voice. "So it was not Lord Fairchild who has overset you like this," she said to herself slowly. "What, then, I wonder could it be?"

Miss Winley turned away and blinked rapidly. She was, Mrs. Merriweather thought, close to shattering. She placed a gentle hand on the young girl's arm.

"Won't you tell me, my dear? Perhaps I can help. I am very good at that. And," she added, "very discreet. What you tell me I shall tell no one, including your mother, if that is what you wish."

For a moment, matters hung in the balance, then desperation won. Tears spilled over and down the girl's cheeks. "Yes, I think I should like that," she said. "But not here."

"No," Mrs. Merriweather agreed, "not here. My room is nice and snug and private and no one will think to disturb us there."

A tremulous smile and a slight nod of the head were all the answer Miss Winley gave. But it was enough. Mrs. Merriweather turned and led the way.

The day grew even stranger as a steady stream of callers arrived that afternoon. One said he had been promised by Lord Fairchild a chance to purchase his favorite hound, another his favorite mount, a third his new curricle. Fairchild developed an increasingly harried look upon his face as the day wore on and he had to constantly dissuade his callers from forcing him to carry through on these proposed bargains.

He was entirely routed, however, when an elderly,

rather corpulent neighbor shook his hand and thanked him for making him happy by telling him that Pamela was willing to be his bride.

"No! No, I tell you! It was the spirits talking last night," Lord Fairchild all but shouted.

The neighbor blinked. "But you seemed sober enough at the time. I even asked to be sure."

Lord Fairchild shook his head. "Doesn't matter. I was three sheets to the wind. Or in a wild humor. Either way, I was not serious. I cannot have been. In any event, Pamela will marry no one just yet, and when she does, I hope she will choose someone more her own age."

"Dash it all, Fairchild," the neighbor said, with pardonable anger, "you cannot tell a fellow he may marry one day and take it back the next." He wagged a finger. "I'll tell you what it is. You're mad, utterly mad. Or dashed cruel!"

And then the fellow crammed his hat back onto his head and strode out the door. Lord Fairchild fled in the opposite direction, telling his wife, over his shoulder, "I am not at home anymore this afternoon. And if anyone else claims I promised him a bargain, fob him off. Tell him I was mistaken. Anything! But I cannot take any more!"

Mrs. Merriweather and Lady Fairchild watched him go and then looked at one another with patent confusion in their eyes. "I think perhaps I shall tell Damford to tell any further callers that none of us are at home this afternoon," Lady Fairchild said carefully.

"I think," Mrs. Merriweather answered just as carefully, "that would be an excellent notion."

Then, because her former pupil seemed close to tears, Mrs. Merriweather took her hand and squeezed it with compassion. "It will all come about," she said.

"How?" Lady Fairchild whispered.

"I don't know, but it will," Mrs. Merriweather promised. "It must!"

Chapter 7

It was the one maid, entering the library to look for another maid, the next morning, who discovered the body. Her shriek penetrated through the entire household, startling even the maid who was supposed to be clearing out the ashes in the grate in the library but was instead sharing the embrace of the third undergroom in a darkened hallway.

Naturally the sound of shrieking brought the major domo to the scene. And any number of susceptible female servants and footmen. It was the housekeeper who finally had the presence of mind to say to Damford, "P'rhaps I'd best inform her ladyship that his lordship is dead."

That recalled the fellow to himself and he said, "Yes, yes, you should indeed do that, Mrs. Breen. It will come as a grave shock to her ladyship I fear. As for the rest of you," he added, drawing himself to his full height and regarding the cluster of servants with a frosty eye, "you've all work to do and should return to doing it. At once!"

That caused everyone to scatter. Mrs. Breen slowly mounted the stairs, thinking to herself that it was a wonder anyone could have slept through the maid's shrieking, but patently the family had. She also found herself wondering how her ladyship would deal with the shock of what she was about to tell her.

As it was, however, it was Mrs. Breen who suffered

the profound shock. She rapped at the bedroom door
in question and it opened almost at once.

"Yes?" Lord Fairchild demanded in a rather impatient voice. "What the devil is it? And what was that
caterwauling downstairs, just now?"

But Mrs. Breen did not answer his questions. She
stared at him. Her face turned bright red, then ex-
tremely pale. She stammered. "B-b-but you're dead!"

And then she fainted. Lord Fairchild fortunately
had the presence of mind to catch Mrs. Breen before
the poor woman hit the floor but that was all he could
think to do. He stood there holding her, calling for
his wife, hoping she would have some notions to the
point.

Lady Fairchild took one look at the housekeeper,
listened to her husband's rather incoherent explanation, then promptly took charge. Even in her night
rail and robe she was a formidable force.

"Place her in that chair, over there. Yes, that one
will do. Now ring for a servant. Dead, you say? She
told you that you were dead? How very odd, to be
sure. Do you think she has been drinking? Never
mind, we shall ask her all about it when she comes
around. And did she say what the shrieking was
downstairs?"

"No. Creature fainted before she had the chance,"
Fairchild retorted.

A maid arrived at the door of the room, swiping at
her eyes, and it was evident she had been crying. All
her tears were forgotten, however, when she stared
at Lord Fairchild and promptly went into a shrieking
fit herself.

As Lady Fairchild steered the girl to yet another
chair, Lord Fairchild demanded, "Has the entire
household lost its wits? What the devil is going on?"

Lady Fairchild did not bother to answer him but
instead directed herself to the task of soothing the
hysterical maid and the housekeeper, who was begin-

ning to revive. This task took several minutes but in the end she succeeded. As the maid hiccoughed, the housekeeper was finally able to speak with some coherence.

"Oh, m'lady! Never did I think to see this day! The master, lying dead in the library."

"Yes, but he is not dead," Lady Fairchild said soothingly. "He is right here with me."

"But then who's the body in the library?" the maid demanded, with pardonable confusion.

"That," Lady Fairchild said briskly, "is what I am about to find out. *If* there is a body in the library. Ten to one it is all a misunderstanding. Someone playing a poor jest on the household."

And with that she led what soon became a procession down to the library. Lord Fairchild came with her, of course, as did the housekeeper and the maid. By now a few of the family had roused and scrambled into clothing of one sort or another and they followed as well, asking questions neither Lord nor Lady Fairchild chose to answer. And of course every servant who saw Lord Fairchild, alive and well, could not help but follow to discover what was going on.

It was therefore quite a crowd that gathered at the door of the library. A door Damford had had the presence of mind to lock and set a footman to guard. That meant the major domo had to be found to produce the key and he had been drinking. At the sight of Lord Fairchild he blinked several times and had to be sharply reminded to hand over the key to her ladyship before he did so, with none too steady a manner.

But the Fairchilds had more important things to think about. They could, with a simple order, keep the servants at bay and they did so. But the family members who had followed them downstairs now followed them into the room as well. There the shocking sight of a dead body before the fireplace brought them all to an abrupt halt.

They stared at the body. They stared at one another. But most of all they stared at Lord Fairchild. And back at the body again.

"Extraordinary!" Pamela exclaimed. "Why, he looks exactly like you, Papa. I wonder who he could be?"

And at that innocently phrased question, most of the family promptly scattered, with mutterings about getting dressed and feeling unwell, until it was Pamela and her parents who were left alone in the library. And Mrs. Merriweather. That shrewd woman took one look at the faces before her and sent Pamela upstairs.

"Your parents will need your support and you should be properly dressed when you give it," she told the girl.

It was a measure of the experience of her years as a governess that Mrs. Merriweather's words were enough to send Pamela away. Then the former governess carefully closed the library door and moved very close to Lord and Lady Fairchild so that she could speak in a voice quiet enough not to be overheard by all the interested servants who still hovered nearby in the hallway.

"I collect you are likely to be the magistrate hereabouts, Lord Fairchild. Or your father. But I should suggest calling someone from outside the household to deal with this," Mrs. Merriweather said gently. "And you will need to decide what you will say. No one, seeing this man's face, will believe you are unacquainted with the fellow. So you had best make up your mind to tell the truth."

Lady Fairchild looked from her husband to the body to Mrs. Merriweather and back to her husband again. "It cannot be, can it, Edward?" she asked. "Please tell me it is not your twin brother, Harry. It isn't, is it?"

He looked at her, at the anxious look in her eyes, and he rubbed at his own. He opened his mouth to speak and then closed it again. He smiled a perfunctory smile that did not reach his eyes as he patted her hand.

"No," he sighed.

One word. That's all it was. One word. But the lie, once spoken, could not be taken back. Not when it had been said to his wife. She stared at him and he added, "Harry died years ago. Don't you remember?"

Still Lady Fairchild stared at her husband. For a long moment neither spoke and a silent message seemed to go between them. She turned to Mrs. Merriweather and said, "I depend entirely upon you!"

Then, with her hand covering her mouth, Lady Fairchild turned and fled the room. Mrs. Merriweather, however, was made of sterner stuff. She stayed where she was and stared at Lord Fairchild. He seemed greatly ill at ease under her shrewd scrutiny.

When the library door was once more closed, the diminutive former governess said, in a calm, dry voice, "That was remarkably foolish of you, my lord. Unless you killed this man, it will look far worse for you to lie than if you had told the truth. There must, after all, be other people hereabouts old enough to remember that you had a twin. I certainly do, and unless there is someone else with such a resemblance to you, then everyone, including Anna, will know it must be he, no matter how vehement your denials."

Fairchild turned to her. "There may be any number of family by-blows," he said, tilting his chin up in defiance. "It could be one of those. Jealous and wishing to discover what he might steal."

She shook her head and sighed. "That will do you and your family no good. Your family would look no better if that were the case."

Mrs. Merriweather paused and debated with herself the best way to proceed. Finally she said, choosing her words carefully, "When the magistrate comes, it might be as well, Lord Fairchild, if you were to recall that

it is always foolish to lie about that which can easily
be checked. And it is particularly foolish of you to lie
to me when I wish to help you, if I can.''

He stared at her. Then abruptly he strode past her
out of the room. Mrs. Merriweather watched him go
and sadly shook her head. Anna had told her there
was trouble and here was proof. She had no doubt
that if Andrew knew what was going on, he would
have wished her to return home. But she could not
abandon her former charge now.

With another sigh, Mrs. Merriweather did what she
did best. She took charge. She strode to the door of
the library, pulled it open, spotted the major domo,
and said in a cool, clear voice, "Damford, Lord Fairchild wishes you to send for the nearest magistrate.
The nearest magistrate outside this household," she
amended. "And have him shown into the library directly he arrives.''

And then, before he could ask any questions, she
closed the library door again and turned to study the
room. She was, unlike the family, already dressed and
this might, she knew, be her only chance to examine
the place where the death had occurred.

Marian Merriweather, once that formidable governess known as Miss Tibbles, stood in the middle of the
room and drew on every shred of perception she had
ever possessed. The same faculties she had used to
study a charge's room and discover what mischief the
girl was planning next she now used to study the room
she was in.

Had anything been disturbed? Was there an indica-
tion of whether the dead man had come through the
door or by the window, perhaps? Were there any signs
of a struggle? How had death occurred? What was the
weapon and where might it be found? Was it in the
room or had someone carried it away? And the body?
What distinguished the man from Lord Fairchild? Had
he any unusual features, either in his face or his cloth-

ing? In short, Mrs. Merriweather did everything she could to prepare for the arrival of the magistrate. She hoped he would not be long in coming.

Pamela moved about the gardens without seeing anything. Mama and Papa were inside and refused to speak with her. No one else in the family would speak to her either. She would swear they knew more than they were saying. Her own mind was in a whirl. And now that funny woman Mama had invited to visit appeared to have taken charge. It was she, the servants said, who had sent for Sir Geoffrey, a magistrate.

It was here that Julian found her. He strode into the gardens, his temperament as confident as ever, and he was slapping his riding gloves against one hand.

"I say, Pamela, do you think—"

But he broke off at the sight of her and even dropped his gloves to take her hands. "Pamela! What the devil is wrong? I've never seen you so upset."

But where did one begin and how did one tell anyone, even an old friend, that someone had been killed in your house?

As the moments went on and she still did not answer, Julian grew even more alarmed. He drew her over to a weathered old bench and pulled her down to sit beside him. He pulled her close and tucked her head under his chin and against his chest.

"What is wrong, Pamela?" he repeated. "Whatever it is cannot possibly be as bad as you think. Come, tell me, for we have always helped one another, have we not?"

Now Pamela pulled free and looked up at him, her eyes brimming with unshed tears. "It is indeed as bad as I think, Julian! A dead body has been found in the library!"

"What? Someone died from the food?"

It was a sad attempt at humor and failed signally. Julian tried again, more serious this time. "What was

it, then? Someone go off in a fit of apoplexy? Was it
someone in the family? Is that why you are so overset? Not your father or grandfather, was it?"

Pamela shook her head. "Not apoplexy. Killed."

"Good God! Who?"

"That's just it, Julian. We don't know!" Pamela
wailed, finally giving vent to her emotions. "But he
looks like Papa. Just like Papa! Only no one will tell
me who he could be."

Julian frowned. "Your grandfather's by-blow, perhaps? That would explain why no one will tell you
who it is. Wouldn't be fit for a young lady to know."

He said this firmly, as befitted a young man of the
world. And yet, even to his own ears it sounded fee-
ble. Pamela, however, did not appear to think so. He
could see from the expression on her face that she was
turning the notion over in her mind. At last she spoke.

"Perhaps," she said slowly. "I suppose they would
be reluctant to tell me. But why should the man come
here? And why would he be killed in the library?"

"Asking for money, no doubt."

"But Julian, that would mean someone in the family
killed him!"

At the look on her stricken face, young Deerwood
hastily said, "I may be entirely mistaken. It could just
be a coincidence."

Pamela shook her head. "No, for he looks precisely
like Papa. More so than I should even expect two
brothers to do. Indeed, it was almost like they were
twins. But Papa's brother was killed before I was born.
It cannot be he!"

Julian decided that it would be as well for him to
say nothing more. He could only, he reflected, make
matters worse. So instead he held his childhood friend
while she cried and told him about the shocking events
that had occurred at Kendall Hall since the ball. And
perhaps for the first time in well over a month he did
not think of Catherine Winley at all.

*   *   *

Upstairs, in her rooms, Lady Kendall stood staring out the window. It ought to be raining, she thought. Raining and gloomy, not sunshine and brightness.

A death. In this house. And one brought about by malice, for the poor fellow in the library had not died from apoplexy or any other such natural cause.

A tiny cry escaped Lady Kendall. She had to grip the window ledge to keep herself from running back downstairs. From gathering the dead man up in her arms and searching his face to be sure.

Behind her there was a sound. "Be sensible," someone said.

"Sensible?"

Her voice was harsh even to her own ears, but she did not care. If the man downstairs was who she thought he must be, then she no longer cared for things such as politeness. In her heart a rage was growing.

"Did you know?" she demanded over her shoulder without turning.

"Yes."

"And you didn't tell me?"

"You would have gone to him. Or let him come to us."

Now she whirled around. "And shouldn't we have?" she demanded.

Eyes blazed at her and she took a step backward at their intensity. And at the anger in the voice. "Don't you remember? Don't you remember what it was like? What he was like? The scandal? Would you go back to that time?"

"He was my son."

Her voice broke, and so did the barrier holding back her emotions as she answered. Slowly she sank to the floor crying. The eyes watched her, contempt as strong now as the anger had been moments before.

And then she was alone once more with her grief.

Chapter 8

It was a measure of Damford's distress that Sir Geoffrey Hawthorne was shown into the library, as Mrs. Merriweather had instructed, rather than to a parlor where he could await the Earl of Kendall's or his son, Lord Fairchild's, welcome.

But as he later told Mrs. Breen, the housekeeper, it was perhaps as well that a magistrate should be dealt with by someone who was not entirely a lady herself. Of course, had Sir Geoffrey been arriving as a guest on a social call, it would have been a different matter. But as he was not, it was just as well.

As for Sir Geoffrey Hawthorne, he was rather taken aback to find himself in the library with both a dead body and a lady on her knees, not in grief, as one might have supposed, but engaged in the vulgar task of reaching into the dead man's pockets! She blocked his view of the dead man so that Sir Geoffrey could not see the man's face.

"My good woman, what the devil are you doing?" he demanded.

Completely unabashed, she rose to her feet, dusted her hands together briskly, then looked at him without the least trace of embarrassment or shame in her eyes. Sir Geoffrey was a man of middle height and age, utterly unremarkable in appearance except for his eyes, which held a shrewdness at odds with the rest of his appearance. A shrewdness of which she seemed to take note.

"Good day, sir. I must suppose you to be a magistrate. I am Mrs. Merriweather and I am a guest in this household. I am the one who felt it wisest to send for you rather than allowing anyone here to deal with the matter."

Sir Geoffrey had knit his brows together as he listened to the impertinent woman, but he heard her out. Then, slowly he said, "You seem familiar. Have we met before? I, by the way, am Sir Geoffrey Hawthorne."

It took the woman only a moment to reply. "Why, yes, I do believe we have met. I was governess to a family you knew. My name, then, was Miss Tibbles."

Despite himself and the circumstances of the encounter, Sir Geoffrey grinned. "Miss Tibbles, eh? You were with the Braddocks, weren't you?" When she nodded, he said, "Then I shouldn't find myself surprised by anything you do." At her startled look he added, "Oh, yes, I know all about you. Heard how you dealt with their daughter's temper tantrums. Frogs, wasn't it? And now you've married, I suppose. Merriweather, did you say?"

Mrs. Merriweather had the grace to blush. "Yes, I am married to Colonel Andrew Merriweather and it seems the Braddocks were quite free in talking about me."

Sir Geoffrey made a noncommittal gesture with his hand. He looked at her for a moment and said, "How do you happen to be here? If you are married, then surely you are not still a governess?"

"No, not anymore. But the first girl I was governess to is now Lady Fairchild and she was kind enough to invite me to stay. I do not think she planned on quite this degree of excitement for my visit, however," Mrs. Merriweather concluded in dry tones.

"Ah." Sir Geoffrey nodded. He looked to the body and this time flinched. "Good lord! No one told me it was Lord Fairchild who was dead!"

"Lord Fairchild is alive and well," Mrs. Merriweather said carefully. "The dead man, however, does bear a remarkable resemblance to his lordship, save that he carries a number of scars."

Sir Geoffrey moved closer. For several moments he studied the body in silence, then moved about the room studying it much as Mrs. Merriweather had done such a short time before. He was profoundly grateful that she had the wit to be silent while he did so.

When he finally spoke, it was to ask her, "You have had more time in here than I. What can you tell me about this man? How did he come to be here? Do you know anything about his death?"

Miss Tibbles or, rather, Mrs. Merriweather met his eyes easily. "He bears a scar on his right cheek and another on the left side of his skull. Both, I should judge, were obtained years ago. He bears a marked resemblance to Lord Fairchild. Death appears to be the result of his being stabbed with the letter opener which still protrudes from his back. Very little in the room appears to have been disturbed. It does not look as if there was a great struggle, which would account for the fact that no one heard anything during the night. The dead man does not appear to have entered the room through the window. However, as the servants supposed him to be Lord Fairchild when the body was first found, it would seem he did not come by the front door either or someone would have remarked upon his arrival."

"The servants found the body, you say?"

"One of the maids. Her shrieks roused the entire household this morning," Mrs. Merriweather confirmed.

Again Sir Geoffrey fell silent. Finally he said, "I had best speak with the household, one by one. Do you know who happens to be in residence at the moment?"

"The Earl and Countess of Kendall, their son Lord Fairchild and his wife, the earl's sister Lady Gwendolyn Avery and her children, Richard and Daphne, Miss Fairchild and her youngest brother, myself and my infant daughter, Lady Winley and her daughter Catherine. And the staff, of course."

"Any strangers seen hanging about, of late?" Sir Geoffrey asked.

"None that I know of, but I cannot suppose anyone would be likely to mention it to me if they had."

Sir Geoffrey nodded. He looked around the room again then sighed. "Do you know the household well enough to suggest a room where I might speak with people?" he asked.

"Yes. Let me show you the way. And I have the key to lock this room so that nothing will be disturbed in the meantime."

"Excellent. I always supposed you to be a sensible woman," Sir Geoffrey said.

Mrs. Merriweather merely smiled. She locked the door, as promised, and then led the way to a parlor she had rarely seen used during her visit. It was small but comfortable and seemed almost to invite confidences. Mrs. Merriweather seated herself in a corner where she was not likely to be seen unless one looked for her.

"You ought to ring for Damford, the major domo, and tell him who you wish to speak with first," Mrs. Merriweather suggested.

Sir Geoffrey nodded. Within minutes, both the Earl of Kendall and his wife entered the room. Mrs. Merriweather shrank farther into her chair. She was not surprised to see that the earl was supporting his wife with an arm about her waist. The countess had taken the appearance of a dead body in her household very hard and Marian could not blame her.

"My apologies for disturbing you at such a difficult time," Sir Geoffrey said gently. "I will try to make this as brief as I can. But I do need to know whatever you can tell me about this dead man and how he came to be here."

The countess seemed almost to be in shock. She

only shook her head, or so Marian assumed since she could not see her from her concealed vantage. The earl answered for the both of them.

"This has been a great shock, as you must realize. I knew that I had a number of offspring, born the wrong side of the blanket, hereabouts, but I had no notion any of them resembled my son so closely."

The countess made a small sound of protest. The earl answered her in soothing, apologetic accents, as well he might. "I am very sorry to distress you, my dear. But you must know it has been years since I sought out any other women."

Sir Geoffrey cleared his throat. "So you do not think it could be your other son?"

"Harry? Impossible! You must know he was killed in a duel some fifteen years ago!"

"So I have heard."

"My dear sir, there is really nothing I or Lady Kendall can tell you. I should like to take her upstairs now. This has been very difficult for her."

"I understand completely and I regret the necessity to intrude," Sir Geoffrey replied. "I will have the body removed as soon as possible."

"Removed?"

"Well, I must presume that since you do not know who it is, you will not wish to have it lying about here," Sir Geoffrey said in the most innocent of tones.

There was a moment of silence and it was Lady Kendall who protested. "No! He must be buried here!"

"My wife means that since the man bears such a marked resemblance to my son, Lord Fairchild, that he must be related in some way, even if irregularly so. Therefore, of course, we will wish to take responsibility for his burial. His body may be placed in the family plot, and when his identity is discovered, then a marker may be placed with his name," the earl said, beginning hastily but growing calmer as he reached the end of his little speech.

It was Sir Geoffrey's turn to be silent. After a moment Lord Kendall pressed the point. "I presume you can have no objection, sir."

"No, no, you may do as you wish," Sir Geoffrey agreed. "As you say, there can be no question that in some manner the poor devil was related to your family. It is generous of you to be so kind to a mere by-blow."

Mrs. Merriweather could not see the earl's reaction or that of his wife but she could well imagine he shrugged in a self-deprecating manner.

"Most men, and their wives, would scarcely be so charitable," Sir Geoffrey persisted.

"I am not most men," the earl said in a cold voice. "Nor is my wife most women."

"No, sir. Of course not."

Mrs. Merriweather could not decide whether Sir Geoffrey meant to be sarcastic or sincere. Apparently the earl and countess did not know either. After a moment, she heard them leave. Both she and the magistrate listened as Lord Kendall called for Damford and ordered him to send someone to fetch the vicar so funeral arrangements could be made. Neither spoke to the other, and Mrs. Merriweather did not move from her chair. Not even when the voices faded away and Sir Geoffrey rang for someone to fetch Lady Gwendolyn for him.

It took some time to find the earl's sister and she arrived flanked by both her children. Sir Geoffrey made no protest when she suggested that he speak to them all at once. Mrs. Merriweather stayed where she was and listened.

"Thank you for agreeing to see me," Sir Geoffrey said, for all the world as though the woman had a choice. "I am hoping you can help me discover the truth about this sorry business. Have you any notion who the dead man might be?"

"It is obviously a stranger, one who can have no

connection to us," Lady Gwendolyn pronounced with a distinct sniff. "I wonder why you are wasting your time talking to us. You ought to be speaking to the servants and discovering which female servant was expecting an admirer or which male servant was allowing one of his friends to make free of the house. There is nothing I or my children can tell you."

Sir Geoffrey cleared his throat. "Forgive me, Lady Gwendolyn, for being indelicate but the dead man greatly resembled Lord Fairchild. I'm afraid that I must ask you if you are aware of any family offspring born the other side of the blanket?"

Lady Gwendolyn evidently gave him an outraged look for Mrs. Merriweather heard Sir Geoffrey hastily say, "No, of course you would not. My apologies, Lady Gwendolyn. Er, perhaps you could at least tell me of the late Lord Fairchild? The one killed in a duel?"

"We do not," Lady Gwendolyn said in an austere voice, "speak of that appalling fellow."

"Just so," Sir Geoffrey agreed. "Quite natural, of course, given his reputation at the time."

"Surely, sir," Richard broke in to say, "there is no need to question us further. We have no notion who the fellow is or how he came to be in the house or how he came to be murdered, for that matter."

"We should like to be of assistance," Daphne added in a helpful voice, "but we simply can't."

Mrs. Merriweather heard Sir Geoffrey sigh. "Very well. You may go. I had merely hoped that someone might have heard something that would be of use to me."

None of the Averys took the bait. Instead they left the room quietly. Sir Geoffrey waited a moment before he requested the next individuals to be brought to him. He did not speak his thoughts aloud nor did Mrs. Merriweather speak hers. They simply waited to see what would be said next.

Chapter 9

Unaware of Sir Geoffrey's arrival, Catherine Winley and her mother were upstairs packing. "I cannot and will not stay in a household so poorly run as this!" Lady Winley pronounced. "I have never before had to deal with anything so shocking as a dead body and, the home of an earl or not, Kendall Hall is not what I have been led to believe it was!"

Her daughter paced the room trying to think of some way to persuade her mother to stay. But she knew it was hopeless. Mama had made up her mind. That was what fueled Catherine's panic.

Just as she had concluded there was no way out, Catherine heard the rap at the bedroom door and she hastened to answer it.

The maid bobbed a curtsey. "If you please, ma'am, the magistrate, Sir Geoffrey, is here and is wishful of speaking to you."

"To me?" Catherine echoed in a bewildered voice.

"Surely she means Sir Geoffrey wishes to speak to me," Lady Winley corrected her daughter tartly.

The maid bobbed another curtsey. "Sir Geoffrey wishes to speak with both of you, I think."

Mother and daughter looked at one another and then, with some reluctance, followed the maid downstairs. They both had a myriad of questions but only Lady Winley voiced hers out loud, not troubling to hide her vexation.

"I cannot think why this Sir Geoffrey should wish

to speak to either of us. Surely it cannot be about the body for we know nothing. Unless perhaps it is mere courtesy because he knows your father? It seems most unlikely for I do not think Winley has ever been to these parts. No, odd as it sounds, this must be about the dead man and that is a great foolishness and will only delay our departure further."

The maid turned at this and said, a hint of smugness in her expression, for Lady Winley was not a favorite in the servants' hall, "Sir Geoffrey is wishful of speaking to everyone about the murder. And they do say he does not wish anyone to leave Kendall Hall."

"That cannot apply to us," Lady Winley said haughtily. "We had nothing to do with that poor man's death. Nor can I think the family will wish us to linger."

"No, ma'am!" the maid said with more fervor than could be accounted for by anything save impertinence. This impression was confirmed when she added, just before she pointed to the small parlor and flounced away, "There, ma'am. Sir Geoffrey wants you in there. And whatever you may want, it's likely you will have to stay, just the same!"

Sir Geoffrey was cordial but calm and somewhat distant as he greeted the two ladies. He listened carefully to the account of how they had come to be invited to stay at Kendall Hall.

"So neither of you is well acquainted with the family?" he asked.

"Naturally not!" Lady Winley replied. "The Winleys have never had anything to do with people being killed. It simply isn't done."

Sir Geoffrey raised a skeptical eyebrow but turned to Catherine. His tone was kinder as he said, "This must be very upsetting to you, my dear Miss Winley, but tell me again how you came to be known to Miss Fairchild."

Catherine colored up and twisted her handkerchief

in her lap. Her mother adjured her to speak up. And most humiliating of all, Sir Geoffrey, with his penetrating gaze said sharply, "The truth now, if you please!"

Someone cleared their throat and for the first time Lady Winley and her daughter realized there was someone else in the room. It was the odd woman who had once been Lady Fairchild's governess. She came forward now and said calmly, "Might I perhaps make this easier by saying no doubt there is a young man involved? And that Miss Winley accepted an invitation she suspected was prompted by his intervention?"

Lady Winley gaped at Mrs. Merriweather but Catherine nodded, relieved to have the matter taken out of her hands. The woman turned to Sir Geoffrey and added, "If one takes into account the ambition of the mother and her not realizing how young the earl's grandsons were, one sees easily how they came to be here."

Sir Geoffrey actually smiled at the odd creature. "Perhaps one does," he acknowledged. "Very well, let us move on to the dead body. Do you know, either of you, who the person might have been?"

Catherine shook her head. "I have not seen the body. I know nothing about it."

"And you, Lady Winley? Will you also say that curiosity did not bring you downstairs to see the commotion, earlier today?" Mrs. Merriweather asked. "Recollect that Sir Geoffrey has already spoken with almost all of the family and knows what they have had to say."

Lady Winley sighed and conceded the point. "Well, yes, I did come down and I did have a brief glance into the library. But I could see very little. Only that the man appeared to bear an uncanny resemblance to Lord Fairchild. If my daughter were not here, I would speak my mind bluntly on the folly of allowing one's by-blows to hang about the place. It only leads to just such unpleasantness as this."

Sir Geoffrey and Mrs. Merriweather exchanged an odd glance but neither challenged Lady Winley's assessment. Instead he said, smoothly, "I thank you both for your help. I need not tell you, I suppose, that I also depend upon your discretion? And I should be grateful, very grateful, if you would continue to stay at Kendall Hall for a bit longer."

When it was obvious Lady Winley meant to protest, Sir Geoffrey leaned just a trifle closer and said, "It would be of help to me, do you see, to know there is someone here other than family. Someone who might be able to tell me of anything interesting that was overheard."

Lady Winley preened at the notion. It could not but appeal to her malicious side, after all. And so, after a moment she nodded graciously and said, "My daughter and I shall stay out the rest of our appointed visit. But no longer, sir. I cannot have my daughter's chances marred by association with such a nasty business as this."

He nodded and stepped aside to let them leave the room. When they were gone, he turned to Mrs. Merriweather but she merely shrugged. Sir Geoffrey sighed and rang for the maid to summon the next party.

It was evident that someone was protective of the daughter of the household for Miss Fairchild came in accompanied by a young man who defiantly stood behind her chair as she faced Sir Geoffrey.

The magistrate looked to Mrs. Merriweather for enlightenment and she did not fail him. "Mr. Julian Deerwood is a childhood friend. I've no doubt Miss Fairchild has confided in him the events of this morning."

Sir Geoffrey cast a considering eye on the young man. "A childhood friend? Then no doubt you were here at the ball, the other night?"

Mr. Deerwood glared back but he made no attempt

to evade the question. "Yes, of course I was. I left around dawn, as did most of the other guests."

"And you naturally came here today to be of support to your childhood friend, Miss Fairchild, the moment you heard of the goings-on here?" Sir Geoffrey suggested.

The young man flushed. "No, I, that is to say, my reasons for coming over cannot matter. But naturally the moment I heard of the trouble, I wished to be of help to Pamela. Miss Fairchild, that is."

"I see. But you won't tell me why you came? It wasn't perhaps because you already knew of the death?"

Deerwood gaped at him. "How the devil could I have known about that?" he demanded.

Mrs. Merriweather once more intervened. She chuckled mildly and said, "I collect, Sir Geoffrey, that you need look no further than Miss Winley for the cause of Mr. Deerwood's presence here today. You will recall I told you I suspected a young man of being behind the invitation that brought her here?"

One look at both Pamela and Julian's faces sufficed to persuade Sir Geoffrey that Mrs. Merriweather had hit upon the truth of the matter.

"How the devil do you do that?" he demanded, exasperated, despite himself.

Mrs. Merriweather laughed again. "Almost twenty years as a governess teaches one a great deal about young people. More, sometimes, than one would wish to know."

"And teaches one about family secrets?" Sir Geoffrey hazarded.

Slowly Mrs. Merriweather nodded. She was smiling no longer. "Family secrets too," she agreed, her voice sober. "But surely, Sir Geoffrey, it is Miss Fairchild you wish to question right now, is it not?"

"Oh. Er, yes, of course. Now, Miss Fairchild, do you know who the man in the library was?"

"No, sir."

"Had you ever seen him about the place before?"

"No, sir."

"Have you any notion who he might have been? Any guess at all?"

"No, sir."

"I see."

"Sir Geoffrey, is this truly necessary?" Mr. Deerwood objected. "I spoke with Pamela when I first arrived and she told me then she had no notion who the man might be or how he might have come to be killed. Can't you see what this is doing to her?"

Sir Geoffrey and Mrs. Merriweather both turned to Miss Fairchild and caught her looking up at Mr. Deerwood with such a look of longing in her eyes that had he seen it, Julian must have suffered a severe shock. But his gaze was fixed firmly on Sir Geoffrey's face.

The magistrate sighed. "You are right, of course. You may go, Miss Fairchild. But if you do think of anything that might be of use to us, I hope you will come to me. Or to Mrs. Merriweather and confide in her."

Pamela nodded, but no one in the room placed the least dependence on her doing as she had been asked. Mrs. Merriweather escorted her and Mr. Deerwood to the door of the drawing room, and just before the young people would have left, the former governess placed a hand on the girl's arm and said, gently, "I have a great deal of practice in hearing confidences, if it would help."

Again Miss Fairchild nodded, but this time there was a hint of less reserve and Marian allowed herself to believe that perhaps the child would confide in her, if there were anything to confide, of course. Then she and Mr. Deerwood left, closing the door behind them.

So Sir Geoffrey and Mrs. Merriweather were once more alone together. "Well, now what the devil do we do?" he demanded. "We have interviewed every person in this household and not learned a thing to the point!''

Mrs. Merriweather tilted her head to one side. "Perhaps," she said. "And then again, perhaps not. In any event, over the next few days something may be said or learned that will tell us what we need to know."

The magistrate eyed her shrewdly. "There you go again. I never meant, you know, to take you on as a colleague, Mrs. Merriweather. I never meant to allow you to sit in upon these interviews, much less intervene in any of them. But you have done so anyway!"

Marian looked at him calmly. "And have I done anything other than help?"

"No," he conceded. "But it unnerves me, it does. M'late wife was the only other person ever able to do that to me before."

She smiled. "Just be grateful, sir, that you have an ally inside the household. Otherwise I should guess it most unlikely you would ever learn anything."

Sir Geoffrey grumbled but he could not dispute the point. Still grumbling, he took his leave of the household. This was not the sort of thing he had anticipated having to deal with when he became a magistrate, and he didn't like it. He didn't like it one bit.

Neither, had he only known it, did Mrs. Merriweather. But like Sir Geoffrey, she knew her duty and would do it. She only hoped that no one she cared about would get hurt in the process. The trouble was, she could not in the least see how it was to be avoided.

Chapter 10

It was a melancholy group that gathered for dinner that night. And a haphazard dinner that was served. Damford apologized, explaining that the younger servants were given over to hysterics and everything was at sixes and sevens belowstairs.

"I should quite naturally have turned off some of the younger staff and replaced them with more reliable persons had Sir Geoffrey not asked that no one leave the premises for the time being," Damford added, clearly mortified at this turn of events.

The Earl of Kendall waved a hand at him. "Never mind, Damford, you've done your best. We can all see that. It's to be understood, indeed expected, that some of the staff would be upset today. But you'll have things back to normal in no time, I daresay."

Damford bowed, patently gratified at the compliment.

Nothing to the point could be said while the servants were present to serve dinner. And one might have argued that nothing to the point was likely to be said while strangers sat at the table, either. In any event, it was a morose group making a ghastly attempt at normalcy in their conversation and the effort fell sadly flat.

Still, the subject could not be ignored entirely. That would be just as bad, advertising to the servants as it would, that some or all of the persons present knew more than they were saying.

"Beastly business," Lord Kendall said, clearing his throat ostentatiously.

"Indeed," Lady Kendall agreed.

"When is the funeral to be?" Lady Fairchild asked tentatively.

"I do hope we shall not be forced to wear black gloves and go into mourning for what is, after all, the death of a perfect stranger," Lady Gwendolyn added.

This last was considered such an affront to common sense that, for a moment, no one could say a word. As usual, it was Mrs. Merriweather who came to the rescue. In her prosaic voice she said, "I believe I heard someone say that the funeral is to be in four days. Is that not so, Lord Fairchild?"

"Er, yes, quite so."

"But must we hang black bunting and wear black gloves?" Lady Gwendolyn persisted.

Mrs. Merriweather did not, perhaps, feel quite equal to dealing a member of her hostess's family a setdown. In any event she merely looked at her plate. It was Lord Kendall who finally looked at his sister and said, in accents of loathing, "Given that the dead man resembled your nephew so completely, we must presume him to be a relative. So, yes, I should presume black gloves to be called for. And do, Gwendolyn, at least make an attempt to appear grieved that someone has died. Whether you knew the person or not, you ought to feel some grief at the death of a fellow creature."

But Lady Gwendolyn bristled at this setdown. "How do we know the fellow didn't deserve to die?" she demanded. "He couldn't have been a very savory sort of fellow or he would never have gotten himself into such a mess in the first place! Well," she demanded when no one quite had the temerity to reply to such an outrageous statement, "would he?"

Lady Kendall looked very pale and near to fainting. More than one family member wondered that she should have come downstairs to dinner instead of taking a tray in her room. Now she rose to her feet, signaling the end of the meal.

"Ladies, shall we retreat to the drawing room?" she said in her well-bred voice that no one had ever heard her raise in anger before. It was unmistakably angry now, however, and that anger appeared to be directed at Lady Gwendolyn. When no one moved, she added, pointedly, "Now?"

Everyone but Lady Gwendolyn rose to their feet with alacrity. She joined the other ladies, but slowly and grumbling every step of the way.

Left alone, the gentlemen looked at one another. The earl repeated the opinion he had given earlier: "This is a bad business. A very bad business indeed."

In reply his son poured himself a healthy dose of brandy and pushed the bottle toward his father. His cousin, Richard Avery, sullenly reached for it third.

"I don't see what all the fuss is about," he said with patent annoyance. "No one cares about a dead stranger. Why was Sir Geoffrey even called here? Asked the most impertinent questions you can imagine!"

Since each of the gentleman had had a turn with Sir Geoffrey, none was inclined to dispute this assessment. Instead they all took another deep sip of brandy.

"It will all blow over, won't it?" Richard persisted. "No one can really suppose any of the family had anything to do with this death, can they?"

The other two men looked at him incredulously, then at each other. Carefully the Earl of Kendall set down his glass. This betrayed to the other two that he had been indulging far more freely than was his usual habit. Neither one blamed him and indeed Lord Fairchild threw back the rest of his brandy and reached for the bottle again himself.

"They will," the earl said with the same care with which he had set down his glass, "find out it was Harry. And then the devil will be in it."

"Harry," Lord Fairchild said with equal care, "died fifteen years ago and the whole world knows it."

"That's right," Richard chimed in stoutly.

The earl snorted. "So we said. So the world believed. But how long do you think that tale will hold now? I don't say we should admit it. Indeed I plan to claim the dead fellow looks like one of my by-blows. But if anyone looks close enough, they'll wonder about Harry. And then we'll all be in for it."

"Then they simply," Lord Fairchild said, leaning back in his chair, "must not have the chance. It's a good thing the funeral is only four days from now."

"How the devil did that woman know that?" Richard demanded. "You cannot tell me you confided in her before telling us, sir," he said to his uncle, Lord Kendall.

"No, I did not," the earl agreed. "I suppose she discovered it the same mysterious way women always find out what we least wish them to know. One must hope she learns nothing more damaging than that. She has, after all, no reason to be loyal to our family. Unless, Edward, your wife can persuade her to discretion."

"I shall speak to Anna tonight."

In the drawing room, the ladies were unusually quiet. Lady Winley and her daughter seated themselves as far away from the others as possible. It was meant as something of a snub but the others felt only relief. Daphne picked up some needlework and busied herself with it, as did Pamela. Lady Gwendolyn perused an issue of *La Belle Assemblée*.

Mrs. Merriweather watched Lady Fairchild closely. She knew only too well those signs of agitation as her former charge paced about the room.

Lady Kendall made no pretense of doing anything. Instead she studied every face in the room, even Mrs.

Merriweather coming under her close scrutiny. Finally she turned her attention to her son's wife.

"Oh, stop pacing, Anna," Lady Kendall finally said, with some impatience. "It will not change a thing."

Lady Fairchild turned to face the countess. "But don't you see?" she asked. "What if the person meant to be killed was supposed to be Edward? What if it was only an accident that this other person was killed instead? That would mean Edward was still in danger."

"No one can possibly be in danger," Lady Gwendolyn pronounced firmly. "We shall not allow it."

Anna looked at her onetime mentor. "Miss Tibbles, what do you think? You were with Sir Geoffrey all day. Ought I to be worried on Edward's behalf?"

Mrs. Merriweather ignored the misstatement of her name. After all, it was understandable that under such provocation as this Anna should revert to the name by which she had known her governess.

"I think," Mrs. Merriweather said, with great care, "that Lord Fairchild ought to be cautious in what he says and does. While we cannot know if he was meant to be the one murdered, prudence would certainly suggest that he proceed as if he might have been."

"There! You see? I am right to be worried!" Lady Fairchild told Lady Kendall with a sense of triumph.

But the countess had heard Mrs. Merriweather's words a trifle differently than had Lady Fairchild. She looked at the former governess with a piercing gaze and said, "You would advise us all to have a caution in what we say and do, wouldn't you, Mrs. Merriweather?"

"I would."

"Why?"

The former governess sighed. "All families have secrets," she said. "And death, particularly violent death, has a way of revealing them. If someone felt strongly enough to kill once, who knows what provocation would be sufficient for that person to do so again?''

The others in the room were spared having to long contemplate such an appalling notion by the arrival of the men, none of whom, it seemed, had wished to linger over their brandy. Anna immediately seated herself beside Mrs. Merriweather, who patted her hand reassuringly.

A halfhearted suggestion was made to set up card tables but it was abandoned for lack of support. Nor was anything more than the most desultory conversation possible. Not when one could not say what was truly on one's mind. It was perhaps no surprise, therefore, that the cluster broke up early as everyone seemed to choose to seek their beds.

Mrs. Merriweather watched them all disperse to their rooms with a crease upon her forehead. Something was very wrong here. But then, of course it was, she scolded herself. If it had not been, a man would not have been murdered. She knew only too well that when matters nagged at her as they did now, sleep would not easily come to her.

So it was that after the rest of the household was quiet, Mrs. Merriweather slipped downstairs and into the library to find a book to read. She had glanced at and discarded the meager selection already in her room. It was of the improving sort and not to her taste, particularly tonight. No, there must be, she told herself, something more inviting in the library. Something sufficiently distracting to take her mind away from the troubles of the household.

She found the room with ease for it was natural to Mrs. Merriweather to note the location of the library of any household in which she found herself. Kendall Hall was no exception. And the walls were indeed lined with all sorts of inviting tomes. Everything from Latin works to novels.

Mrs. Merriweather reached for one of the latter,

thinking to herself that she would be served her just deserts if Anna Fairchild were to find her in possession of the book. Novels had been only one of the battlefields between them when she was governess and Anna the restless and reckless young woman in her charge.

Not quite five years had separated them in age, but Marian had done her best to make them seem greater. She had hidden carefully all the ways in which she identified with the girl and done her best to shape her to pass within the bounds of society successfully. And she had.

Lord Fairchild had met and wooed and wed Anna all in one brilliant Season even though his own brother had courted her as well, which was one reason Mrs. Merriweather remembered Harry's existence after all these years. He had not taken defeat in the matter well.

But Anna had married and Mrs. Merriweather had moved on to the next household, the next girl. In all the years since, she had heard of no trouble between Lord Fairchild and his wife. Until this visit.

Mrs. Merriweather grasped the book in one hand and her candle in the other when something caught her eye. She set down both to peer a little closer at the patch of paneling near the fireplace. It looked oddly familiar, though she had never been in this household before. She tried to recall where the memory came from. An old house, certainly. One that dated back hundreds of years perhaps.

Then she had it! The house she recalled had boasted a number of secretive features. A priest hole. Hidden doorways and cupboards and places to conceal all manner of precious things. And the paneling in the library there had matched this almost exactly. Was that where the first Lord Kendall had conceived the notion? Had he had it copied? How precisely had he had it copied, the former governess wondered.

Curiosity was Marian Merriweather's besetting sin. It was one she had repressed for many years. Except, of course, when she had used it on behalf of her charges. Now she gave way to it just for herself. She could not resist discovering whether this library held hidden places just as that other library, that other paneling, had done.

To her delight, she found it did. She pressed wooden leaves and flowers in the sequence the owner of that other house had shown her and suddenly a door popped open. It was a tiny door, for it hid a small cupboard, not a passageway, but it was a door nonetheless. Mrs. Merriweather could not help giving a small cry of triumph that she had been right and that she had remembered the intricate sequence needed to open the thing.

But it was perhaps that tiny cry that was her error. For though she did not hear it, the library door stealthily opened behind Mrs. Merriweather. And as she reached for the hiding place, simply to close it, you understand, something struck the back of her head and she slumped to the floor. A shadowy figure knelt beside her, then moved swiftly to search the cupboard.

She was not so foolish as to try to sit up or otherwise give away her lucid state. But something must have alerted the person anyway. The person became frantic, not finding what was expected there. He or she, for Mrs. Merriweather was too addled to tell which it was, came to kneel again beside the former governess and demand hoarsely, "What did you find? What did you take?"

When she did not at once answer, the figure started to shake her. And that dissolved the last vestiges of Mrs. Merriweather's strength. She slipped into a not entirely unwelcome unconsciousness.

Chapter 11

"Miss Tibbles? Miss Tibbles? Oh, please, Miss Tibbles, you must be all right! I shall never forgive myself if you are not!"

Mrs. Merriweather struggled to answer the poor woman. Only no sound would come out of her mouth and her eyes seemed unaccountably reluctant to open.

Another voice, a younger female voice, said with patent concern, "There is a great deal of blood. Perhaps we ought to send for a physician."

Still another voice, the Earl of Kendall's, said imperiously, "What the devil was the woman doing in here, anyway? Impertinent creature. Most of our houseguests do not have the temerity to wander about the place and get themselves attacked like this!"

Had Marian been able to do so, she would have pointed out to Lord Kendall the infelicity of such a remark. But someone else did so for her. And then that person added, "Well, at least this ought to prove to Sir Geoffrey that we are subject to intruders. The window is wide open!"

But the person who struck her had not come through the window, Mrs. Merriweather thought with a frown. She tried to say so, but again her voice would not comply.

Someone else said, a trifle querulously, "But what about a physician? Oughtn't we to send for a physician?"

That caused a flurry and Mrs. Merriweather could hear the necessary orders being given. She would have protested, had it been possible, for she was not enamored of physicians. But once again she found herself silent. A moment later, however, she found that she could, at least, open her eyes.

The moment she did so, Mrs. Merriweather realized that every member of the household must be crowded into the library. But scarcely had she done so than a clear, cold voice said, "Everyone out. Anna, you may stay with Mrs. Merriweather until the physician arrives, but everyone else is to leave the room. The poor woman can scarcely breathe with everyone crowding around her so."

Lady Kendall. Marian recognized the voice. And the tone of authority. She was very grateful for it for within moments the room was empty of all save herself and Lady Fairchild. To be sure, Lady Kendall herself paused in the doorway and regarded Mrs. Merriweather with a cold, harsh stare, but then she, too, was gone and the door closed, giving them welcome privacy.

"Miss Tibbles, what on earth happened?" Anna asked, helping her former governess to a nearby chair.

"Someone struck me on the back of the head," Mrs. Merriweather replied, reluctant to say more.

"I would not for the world have had this happen to you! I did not think, when I invited you to visit, that any such misfortune could or would befall you here," Lady Fairchild persisted. "Did you see who it was? Did the intruder come through the window?"

Mrs. Merriweather hesitated. Had there been anyone else to overhear, she would certainly have kept her own counsel. But they were alone and perhaps Anna's own safety was at stake. Still, a natural caution made her hesitate beyond the point where it could be ignored.

Lady Fairchild rose to her feet and took a step away. As though she sensed the other woman's caution, she lowered her own voice to say, "So the in-

truder did not come through the window. Otherwise
you would not have hesitated to say so. That must
mean it was someone from our household. Did you
see who, Miss Tibbles?"

Mrs. Merriweather again did not trouble to try to
correct her former pupil. What did it matter, after all,
by what name Anna called her? "I did not see," she
said, keeping her voice pitched low. "But you are
right, the intruder did not, could not have come
through the window. It rained tonight but I'll wager
there are no footprints beneath the windowsill. No
trampled bushes moving away from the house. At
least not yet. I'll not vouch for what will be found out
there in the morning."

Anna nodded. "Yes, I understand. There will be
time enough to provide proof of an intruder, if that is
what someone wishes to do. And to suggest that someone look now would require that one knew who to
ask. You would tell me if you remembered more? If
you remembered something that would identify your
attacker?"

Again Mrs. Merriweather hesitated and Lady Fairchild's voice was bitter as she said, "I see. So you
would not."

"I might or I might not," Mrs. Merriweather corrected her with a gentleness that only those who knew
her well would expect of her. "It would depend upon
what I remembered and who I thought to be at fault.
It would also depend on why I believed the attack
occurred."

"Why did it occur?" Lady Fairchild asked. "And
what were you doing in the library?"

Mrs. Merriweather explained. About wishing for a
book to read, about recognizing the woodwork. About
pressing carved leaves and flowers to reveal a hidden
space. As she spoke, Anna followed her instructions
and, within moments, had opened the cunning door.

The space was now empty and the two women looked at each other.

"What does it mean?" Lady Fairchild asked.

"That," Mrs. Merriweather retorted, not troubling to hide the acid tones in her voice, "is something I fear I cannot answer. Someone took great care to make certain I could not. And I should not like to hazard a guess for I do not think it would be healthy or wise."

She did not add that whatever it was the person wanted, it was gone already by the time he or she had discovered Mrs. Merriweather standing in front of the open cupboard.

Pamela hung back. She did not like to be the center of a scene, in any event, and it was of particular importance that she guard the small parlor door. It would be fatal were Catherine and Julian to emerge into this crowd.

Why, oh, why had she agreed to arrange an assignation? And tonight of all nights when Mrs. Merriweather was attacked? She wished she could go into the parlor and warn her friends, but her courage failed her at the thought. She had not known how hard it would be to watch Julian court Miss Winley. She had not known, until she did, how deeply her own feelings had somehow come to be engaged.

She had always loved Julian but thought it was childish admiration. She had not known her feelings went so deep. And now she could not bear the thought of walking into the parlor and perhaps risking interrupting their embrace.

The door behind her creaked and Pamela realized she could put off matters no longer. Swiftly she moved backwards and slipped inside the door, just as it began to open.

"Pamela! What the devil?"

"*Shhhh,* Julian. And Miss Winley. There is a great

crowd in the hallway, and if you do not wish to be discovered, you must be quiet. It might even be best, Julian, if you were to leave by the window."

"Window?"

"What has happened?" Catherine asked in a practical voice.

"One of the houseguests, Mrs. Merriweather, has apparently been attacked in the library. Everyone is crowding around in the hallway, talking and speculating and waiting for the physician."

"Well, then I may safely slip out into the hallway and pretend that I have come down out of curiosity too," Catherine persisted, in the same practical voice as before.

Julian started to protest but Miss Winley waited for neither their approval nor disapproval; she simply slipped out of the parlor and into the hall.

"How odd!" Pamela could not help but exclaim.

She looked to Julian but he seemed oddly abashed and refused to meet her eyes. She wanted to ask if something were amiss but did not dare. Instinct told her that, being a man, Julian would not welcome such impertinence.

But she misjudged him. Even as she watched, he took a deep breath and lifted his head. "I do not like this," he said. "I do not like such goings-on as dead bodies and attacks on helpless women. I wish that you and Catherine were safely away from here!"

Miss Winley. Of course he would speak of her. Now it was Pamela who looked down at the floor. And twisted her hands together. "No doubt Lady Winley will remove her daughter to a safe place as soon as may be," she said.

Pamela felt rather than saw him move toward her. Suddenly her upper arms were grasped by his strong hands. "And what about you?" he demanded. "Who will have the presence of mind to worry about your safety?"

She looked up at him and almost felt her heart stop as she saw the concern in his eyes. Surely, she told herself, it was just for someone he thought of as a younger sister.

"I- it does not matter," she managed to say.

He shook her. "But it does! I ought to take you out of here, now, and to my home."

Despite herself, despite the intensity of her emotions or, perhaps, because of them, she laughed. Affronted, he let go of her arms and Pamela rubbed them without noticing she did so. Her concern was, instead, to reassure him.

"I was not laughing at you, Julian. I was laughing at the notion of what our families would think. Your mother would be appalled if you showed up with me in the middle of the night, and mine would likely think we had eloped!"

He tried to regard her with disapproval but Pamela knew him too well to believe it. She saw the moment the corners of his mouth began to twitch upward. Understood the instant his own lively sense of humor was engaged. And then he was laughing with her.

"You are right, of course," he said, waving them both to a seat, side by side on the sofa, "but what are we to do? I cannot simply leave you here in danger."

She took his hand. "But I am not in danger. At least I don't think so. I know nothing of what is going on."

"That did not protect Mrs. Merriweather," he replied with a grimness that found an echo in her breast.

"I am not so certain," Pamela said cautiously. "She was with Sir Geoffrey as he questioned each member of the family. And Mama says that when Mrs. Merriweather was her governess, she had a way of knowing everything that went on in the household. Perhaps someone believes she knows too much now. Truly, Julian, I do not think I am in danger."

He regarded her for a long moment with an expression she could not fathom. She tried to withdraw her hand from holding his but he gripped it tight. At last he said, with some emotion she could not name, "If at any time you should feel in danger, send for me. At once!"

When she hesitated, he persisted, squeezing her hand and leaning toward her. His voice was harsh as he said, "Promise me, Pamela!"

She tilted her chin upward. It was the only way to prevent being overcome with emotion herself. She tried levity. "Shall I also send for you, Julian, if I think Miss Winley in danger?"

"Miss Winley? Oh. Yes. Of course. Send for me if either of you is in danger," he said, looking for all the world as if she had suddenly shaken him out of a trance.

"If I promise to do so, will you leave?" Pamela asked. "And by the window?"

In answer, Julian went and put his ear to the parlor door. He came back over to her and sighed. "They are still talking in the hallway. Very well, out the window I shall go. It is not, after all, as though it were the first time I have done so in this house."

They grinned at each other, recollecting childhood mischief. And then they moved toward the window, in perfect accord once again. It was a matter of moments to open the window, allow Julian to slip out into the night, and then close it again behind him. Finally, when she was certain he was safely away, Pamela slipped back out into the crowd of people and waited to learn how seriously injured Mrs. Merriweather might be.

"We must get you upstairs to bed," Anna said firmly as she closed the secret cupboard. "I do not care what was in there so much as I care for your health and safety. Come, if you put your arm about my shoulder, do you think you might manage the stairs?"

But before Mrs. Merriweather could answer, the door to the library opened once more and a rather harried-looking fellow hurried in. It was apparent, from the way his clothing had been fastened slightly askew, that the poor man had been roused from his bed. Now he blinked as he looked from Lady Fairchild to Mrs. Merriweather.

"I am told someone was injured?"

"Yes, my guest, Mrs. Merriweather," Lady Fairchild said, gesturing toward Marian.

There was a note of indignation in Lady Fairchild's voice, and before she could explain, Mrs. Merriweather made haste to forestall her. In what might have passed, for those who didn't know her, as a vapid voice, she said, "It is the most stupid thing! I appear to have fallen and struck the back of my head!"

"Well, well, let me see," the physician said, moving forward. He inspected the relevant portion of Mrs. Merriweather's head and shook his own. "How did you manage to do that?" he demanded.

Again Lady Fairchild would have answered, and again Mrs. Merriweather forestalled her. "Oh, I scarcely know, sir. One moment I was reaching for a book, the next lying on the floor."

The poor man looked confused, as well he might. He began to ask her about previous fainting spells and such. Finally, with another shake of his head he said, "The injury does not appear to be serious. This time. But in the future I beg you will be more careful, Mrs. Merriweather. A blow to the head can have the most severe consequences."

He then turned to Lady Fairchild and gave her a number of instructions for the care of her houseguest. She thanked him and both women watched him go. When the door had once again safely closed behind him, Lady Fairchild turned a severe eye upon Marian.

"Miss Tibbles, you taught me that falsehoods were never to be tolerated!"

If she thought to discompose her former governess, Anna was mistaken. Mrs. Merriweather met her gaze squarely and said, her voice brisk and most unlike the one in which she had answered the doctor, "And in general they are not. But this is a matter, quite literally, I should say, of life and death and I do not think we wish to advertise abroad the events in this household. Which telling the physician would most certainly do. Now come, help me upstairs and we may both seek our beds."

Lady Fairchild moved with alacrity to assist. But Mrs. Merriweather paused in the act of rising. "Where is the book?" she asked with a frown.

"Book?" Anna echoed warily.

"Yes, I was holding a book when I was struck from behind," Mrs. Merriweather explained.

"Perhaps," Anna said thoughtfully, "whoever struck you thought that that was what you had removed from this hiding place."

The two women looked at each other and Mrs. Merriweather slowly nodded. "I should wager you have the right of it. Well, I wish him or her well of it for it was simply a book I chose from the shelves."

"Can I get you another?"

"No, for my head aches abominably and I cannot think myself in any condition to read tonight. Time enough tomorrow to choose another book. But during the daytime, I think!" she concluded with an attempt at humor.

Anna smiled, but in a most perfunctory way. "You jest," she said, sliding an arm around Mrs. Merriweather's waist, "but I assure you that I should be far happier if you did choose a book during the day. Preferably with someone to watch over you as you do so. I shall ask my daughter to stay by your side. That way no one shall have the chance to finish what they began. I would do so myself but I had arranged to visit the vicar's wife tomorrow and both Edward and I are agreed that it would be a mistake to cry off. But Pamela may stay by your side."

Mrs. Merriweather would have protested, as much on the poor girl's behalf as her own, save that it occurred to her that there might be no better way to discover what was happening in this household. A young girl would not yet have been told all the family secrets. No, nor known precisely how she ought to guard her tongue. She might well let slip what an older, more experienced member of the family would know to conceal. So she merely thanked Anna with a meekness that caused the woman to regard her with the gravest suspicions.

"I shan't ask why you are not protesting," Lady Fairchild said, as they made their way to the library doorway, "for I doubt very much I should like the answer. Unless, of course, you are more severely injured than either the phsyician or I realized. For the moment, at least, I shall be content to see you to your bed."

Outside the library, a large, strong footman waited, as did Lord Fairchild. "Peter will carry Mrs. Merriweather upstairs to her room," Fairchild proclaimed. "Even I can see she ought not to try to manage the stairs."

It was a measure of her weakened state that Mrs. Merriweather made no protest. She allowed herself to be gently picked up and carried as though she were a mere trifling thing. It was not an altogether unpleasant sensation, she had to allow. Particularly as her head still ached abominably and she felt what could easily have become a serious lowering of her spirits.

Lady Fairchild followed and fussed a bit, as did Mrs. Merriweather's maid, Kate, who was appalled to discover what had occurred. But eventually the former governess found herself thankfully alone and she lay for some time deep in thought as her candle guttered low. And if a part of her wakefulness had as its reason a fear that her unknown attacker might try again, she had too much resolution of spirit to acknowledge such a thing, even to herself.

Chapter 12

Pamela was still in bed, sipping hot chocolate, when her mother entered her bedroom. Lady Fairchild dismissed the maid and then sat on the chair next to the bed.

This was sufficiently unusual that it caused Pamela to ask, with some uncertainty, "What is wrong, Mama?"

"There is something I wish you to do," her mother said, with a small smile. "I should like you to stay by Mrs. Merriweather's side today. All day."

"Of course, Mama," Pamela said, too relieved that her mother had not come to chastise her for Julian's visit to cavil at such a simple request. "But why? Is she still feeling poorly from last night?"

For a long moment Lady Fairchild stared at the wall above her daughter's head. For a long moment she did not answer. And then she looked Pamela straight in the eyes and said, "I fear for Mrs. Merriweather's safety. I am not convinced that she was attacked by someone outside this house. And because I do not believe anyone would attack you, I think your presence will be sufficient to protect her."

"Mine?"

Pamela laughed, but it was a very uncertain laugh. Lady Fairchild did not even smile now. "I would not ask you if I thought there was any possibility of danger to yourself. I think that whoever did this acted foolishly and without forethought and because there seemed no risk of discovery. If so, then even one pair of eyes would be enough to deter another attack. Perhaps there is no reason to think the villain will try again. But for the moment I should like you to stay by Mrs. Merriweather's side."

"But why me? Why not you?" Pamela asked, still bewildered.

The look in her mother's eyes frightened her more than ever. And Lady Fairchild's words only made it worse. "Because I must pay some morning calls today. I shall spend some time with her, of course, but you must be with her the rest of the day." She paused then added resolutely, "It is more than that, of course. If I am wrong," she said in measured tones, "then I can think of no one better suited to protect *you* than the woman I knew as Miss Tibbles."

And without another word of explanation, Lady Fairchild rose to her feet and glided from the room. Yes, *glided* was precisely the right word and Pamela wasted a moment in crossly wishing she could acquire that particular talent. It was one that Miss Winley also possessed and that gentlemen, such as Julian, seemed to admire.

But she shook off her megrims quickly and threw back the covers. Too much was happening, Pamela decided, to waste her time in bed. No, she had best wash and dress and descend to the breakfast parlor. For Mama had neglected to say when Mrs. Merriweather would rise, but Pamela had noticed the woman was the last person one could call a slug-a-bed and had preceded most of the household down to breakfast every morning since her arrival.

Nor was Pamela mistaken. She was just at the top step of the staircase when Mrs. Merriweather appeared at her elbow. The woman looked Pamela over, head to toe, and nodded with what appeared to be approval.

"I collect we are to be companions, at least for the

day, Miss Fairchild," Mrs. Merriweather said dryly. "Shall we go down to breakfast?"

"Yes, of course. Would you like to take my arm?" Pamela asked.

The woman straightened, her expression turned glacial, and Pamela hastened to add, "I realize that under normal circumstances you would never require such assistance. It is just that you still look a trifle pale this morning. But forgive me if I seem impertinent."

That caused the woman to pause, even as she had opened her mouth to ring a peal over the younger woman's head. Or so Pamela's fevered imagination believed. But then Mrs. Merriweather tilted her head to one side and smiled. She reached out and put a hand on Pamela's shoulder.

"I think, my dear, that perhaps I shall accept your support, after all."

Not wishing to ask what had caused the woman to change her mind, Pamela merely gave her the requested support and they began down the stairs. But Mrs. Merriweather answered her anyway.

Halfway Mrs. Merriweather paused and said softly, "It is always wise, Miss Fairchild, when one is not certain if one is in the presence of enemies, to allow others to underestimate one. Remember that, my dear, should you ever find yourself in uncertain circumstances."

All that Pamela could think of to say was, "I shall."

Mrs. Merriweather nodded to herself, as though satisfied. But the more Pamela thought over those words, the more sensible they seemed. And certainly no one, seeing the woman this morning, would possibly think her a threat. She seemed to have aged and become frail in the moment she decided to accept Pamela's support. And even though she had seen the transformation, it still had the power to confound Pamela and almost cause her to believe in it as well.

But there was strength in the hand that gripped her

arm. There was shrewdness and intelligence in the eyes that surveyed the breakfast room as they arrived. Pamela found herself looking at the assembled family members and houseguests with a new and almost jaundiced eye herself. Someone here might have attacked Mrs. Merriweather, Pamela realized.

She did not believe, nor she was certain did anyone else, the nonsensical tale of a housebreaker. No, it was far more likely that someone in this household— servant, family, or guest—had attacked the woman beside her. And Pamela shivered as she wondered who it might be.

The shiver did not go unnoticed. At least not by Mrs. Merriweather, who pinched her arm. Immediately Pamela recalled herself and helped the woman into a chair and then tried to pretend everything was as it ought to be. And that she had no suspicions of anyone.

Fortunately the attention of everyone in the room was focused on Mrs. Merriweather. There were solicitous questions as to her condition. Offers of various delicacies to tempt her appetite. And a request, when she felt stronger, to tell them precisely what had occurred the night before. And through it all, Mrs. Merriweather continued to play the part of meek and weakened older woman. But Pamela watched where her gaze rested, and for how long. And she began to wonder about some of the people in this room.

Julian Deerwood stared up at Kendall Hall. Situated as it was on a slight rise, it seemed more massive than it really was. And cold and forbidding, for all it had been built in modern times.

Was Pamela all right? he wondered. Did he dare go up to the hall and ask? But what excuse could he give? He could not betray that he had been in the house the night before and already knew about the attack on Lady Fairchild's former governess.

He could, of course, pretend to be calling upon Miss Winley, but then he might not have the chance to talk with Pamela alone. She had seemed frightened the night before, and he wished to assure her again of his support.

In the end, Julian decided to do what he had often done before. He would, he decided, go around to the flower gardens and wait on a bench among the roses. It was her favorite place to go when she was troubled and surely, sooner or later, she would come out there today.

Satisfied with himself, Julian moved toward his destination.

Catherine Winley stared in the looking glass. Was that a haggard look about her eyes? Would anyone wonder at it? Surely not today when much of the household must be short of sleep. Still, she was reluctant to quit her bedchamber.

Each day that she stayed here brought Miss Winley less and less comfort. Each day made clearer the dilemma before her. For a moment she wished she might see Mr. Deerwood again today. But that was foolishness itself and would only bring her more trouble than anything else.

No, she must go downstairs and pretend nothing troubled her. She must go downstairs and pretend to be the innocent creature they thought her to be. And if that thought threatened to bring on a flood of tears, why then Catherine must only hold more firmly to her resolve to prevent discovery at all costs.

Perhaps the garden, she thought. Mama would keep to the house and so would everyone else, no doubt. Surely today even Miss Fairchild would stay indoors, and after last night she did not think Mr. Deerwood would come to see her. Out in the garden she might be alone with her thoughts.

So Catherine Winley moved, with a stealth perfected over the past six months, down the hallway to the stairs and out the side door to the gardens. Only when she was well away from the house did she allow herself a sigh of relief. And then she saw Julian Deerwood.

"Catherine!" he called and came toward her. "I did not dare to hope I might see you today."

She half turned away, but that would have been the coward's course. She made herself stand still and kept her voice cool and calm as she replied, "I did not think to see you here, either. All that needed to be said was said last night, I thought."

He reached for her hands and she put them behind her even as he asked, "Surely that was a misunderstanding?"

"Misunderstanding? Is that what you gentlemen call it these days?"

He flushed and Miss Winley was gratified to see it. She pressed her advantage. "Did you not think of my reputation, should anyone intrude? Did you not think of my feelings? How dare you believe you might use me as you wished? How dare you behave as though I were the veriest strumpet?"

"But it wasn't that at all!" he protested and tried again to reach for her.

Miss Winley took a step backward. Her color was high but her voice firm as she said, "No? Then tell me how it was. Tell me why I should ever speak to you again."

His voice came soft and low and coaxing. "Because I love you. Because I regret what I did. Because I know we are meant to be married."

"You are very sure of that," Miss Winley told him, proud to hear that her voice was steady. "But I am not. I bid you good day, sir. Perhaps Miss Fairchild can explain your error to you, if you cannot see it for yourself."

"As though I should tell her!"

What he would have done next, Miss Winley dared not think, for she knew she had pushed him past his limit. But there was a sound in the shrubbery behind her that neither could mistake, and this time it was Mr. Deerwood who took a step back and pretended an interest in the nearest rose. She stood where she was and waited.

A moment later, Miss Fairchild and the odd little woman, the former governess, emerged from behind the privet hedge and came to an abrupt halt as they spied Miss Winley and Mr. Deerwood.

"Oh, forgive me. I did not realize you were here," Miss Fairchild said, her color high.

"I was just leaving," Miss Winley said, moving to pass the two women.

"Catherine?"

She ignored Deerwood and kept on her way, head held high. She did not know how much had been overheard but she paused, just before passing out of sight, to look over her shoulder and say, "I think perhaps Mr. Deerwood is in need of your counsel, Miss Fairchild. And perhaps even yours, Mrs. Merriweather."

Before any of them could reply, Miss Winley took the necessary step that put her out of sight and moments later began to run. Not toward the house, but even farther away. Somewhere on the grounds was a folly and she meant to find it. For if ever there were a more appropriate refuge for how she felt today, Miss Winley could not think what it might have been.

Left behind, the two women and Julian looked at one another. His color was very high, but his expression was defiant, as though he dared them to ask what Miss Winley had meant. Pamela might have done so, and indeed, Julian thought she would, but Mrs. Merriweather forestalled her.

"I think," she said in a voice that was dry with understanding, "that perhaps we had all best sit down. You, too, Mr. Deerwood. This may take some time.

You may as well know that we overheard a great deal. Not by intention but because it could not be helped."

"You might have gone back the way you came the moment you realized we were in conversation," he flung at her.

The former governess smiled. "We might have, but this seemed far too entertaining. And," she added, seeing that he meant to make a sharp retort, "it seemed that perhaps Miss Winley might need our assistance. Really, Mr. Deerwood, how came you to manage things in such a ham-fisted way? And what, precisely, did you subject her to last night?"

For a long moment Julian stared at his childhood friend, Pamela, and her companion. It was a bitter twist of fate, he thought, that had brought them to this spot in time to overhear his damning words. And he had no doubt how appalling they must have sounded.

He did not care, Julian realized, what the old woman thought. But he did care, desperately, that Pamela should not think so harshly of him. He took a step toward her and was appalled to see her shrink back. That, more than anything else could have done, shocked him into honesty.

He swallowed hard and turned to address Mrs. Merriweather. "I did not do what you apparently think I did," he said.

She raised her eyebrows. In a frosty voice that must have cowed all her charges when she was a governess, the woman said, "Do not presume to tell me what I think, Mr. Deerwood. I asked you a question. Please answer it."

He turned his back on her. "I cannot."

"Why, Julian?" Pamela's voice was scarcely above a whisper. "Did you assault her so badly, then? Go so far beyond the line that you cannot even tell me?"

Shaken, he turned to her and crossed the ground between them. He took her hands in his and this time she did not draw away. Instead she looked up at him, misery patent in her fine green eyes. Her face was pale but she clung to him as he clung to her.

"I kissed Miss Winley. Yes, and proposed marriage, too! I thought we stood upon such terms as made it possible, nay, necessary for me to do so," Julian tried to explain and even he could hear the shaking in his voice. "I did not know she would reject me so thoroughly. She will not even give me the chance to explain."

"Young ladies often are excessively shocked the first time a gentleman kisses them," Mrs. Merriweather observed briskly. "I have also noted, however, that they are far less likely to be shocked, or to object, if they care for the gentleman in question. I must suppose, Mr. Deerwood, your suit to be hopeless."

He would have argued with Mrs. Merriweather. He would have tried to tell her how mistaken she was, she must be, had it not been so important to reassure Pamela instead.

"I pray you will not think me a monster," he said, gentling his voice as much as he was able. "I pray you will not think I offer every young lady such behavior."

Now she smiled bravely and with a slight quiver to her voice she said, "Oh, no, I know you do not for you have never served me such a turn and you have had ample opportunity were you simply of a rakish turn of mind."

Somehow her attempt at bravery, her attempt to smile, cut through Julian more painfully than tears or reproaches could have done. Without thinking, he drew her into his arms and stroked her hair as he murmured soothing words to her.

"I swear I did not mean to cause you pain, Pamela. No, nor to upset a guest under your roof. Your guest. I thought she would welcome my advances. I am more sorry than I can say that I made such a mistake. I swear it shall never happen again. I swear I shall cause you no more pain."

There was a watery chuckle at that, and when he looked down at her, he found Pamela looking up at him with a gleam of mischief in her eyes. "You cannot keep such a promise, you know you cannot."

"I shall try," he averred stoutly.

She pulled free and went to sit beside Mrs. Merriweather, who took her hand consolingly. Now Pamela's voice was distressingly calm as she said, "I know you will try. You always try. And yet you manage to turn things upside down five times out of seven."

The words were harsh, but there was an affection in her voice that lifted Julian's spirits. He grinned back at her and countered, "And you do so seven times out of seven!"

Where their banter might have led, neither found out, for Mrs. Merriweather cleared her throat and said, "I should leave the pair of you alone to twit one another endlessly but I am to stay by Miss Fairchild's side today. So instead why do we not put our heads together and see if we can contrive a way to make matters right with Miss Winley?"

For a moment the name meant nothing to Julian and then he blinked. "Oh. Catherine. Miss Winley. Yes, of course. It is imperative that I make my peace with her."

He could have sworn Pamela winced at his words. But how could that be? She must know how awkward it would be if the strain continued between himself and Miss Winley. And yet, Julian could not feel the relief he ought to have felt to know that so redoubtable a figure as Mrs. Merriweather meant to help him. For the moment, all his thoughts, all his concern, were fixed on Pamela.

Chapter 13

The household was a most depressing one. Black bunting hung from the windows and over the door. The ladies were dressed in black. The servants had taken to moving about in pairs and looking over their shoulders whenever they heard an odd sound. The body had been removed to prepare it for burial, and that was something that could come none too soon for any of them.

The family looked at one another warily and the houseguests were even more open in their discomfort. Both Pamela and her mother, Lady Fairchild, found it oddly comforting to take turns spending time by Mrs. Merriweather's side.

Pamela had not expected to like the former governess, for she had not been fond of her own, so recently dismissed and not yet replaced. Indeed, she had been hoping the woman need not be replaced. But if the new governess were like Mrs. Merriweather, perhaps it would not be so bad, after all. She seemed to be able to see inside one and understand all the things one could not put into words. It was just so as they sat in the garden after Julian left.

"Mr. Deerwood will come about, my dear. Preferably before he entangles himself too many times with other young ladies," Mrs. Merriweather said kindly.

Pamela shook her head. "It cannot be so. Julian thinks of me as though I were a younger sister. Someone he must comfort if she cries and whose welfare he is charged to look out for, but he does not feel any warmer emotion for me."

"And so you have tried to be sensible."

It was not a question. The former governess clearly knew. Now she smiled and patted Pamela's hand. "The trouble with love is, my dear, the heart is not sensible. It will not listen to all the reasonable arguments in the world. If it loves, it loves."

"And if it ought not to love?" Pamela asked, unable to look directly at the woman.

"Then one must put aside the object of one's affection and go on with one's life anyway," Mrs. Merriweather replied. "But even then there is no point in denying the affection. One must face it bluntly and stare it down and only then can one get past it."

"You speak as if you know," Pamela said, realizing too late that perhaps it was an infelicitous remark.

But Mrs. Merriweather only laughed, and when she did so, it was as if she was suddenly years younger. And Pamela could perhaps understand why a certain Colonel Merriweather had fallen in love with her.

"My dear, I do pray you will not try to guard your tongue in front of me!" Mrs. Merriweather said. "I am grateful for your honesty here, in a house that clearly holds so many secrets."

"It does, doesn't it?" Pamela asked eagerly. "I feel it all the time, but especially of late. Of course if I try to ask, I am told it is none of my affair and I ought not to pry into what does not concern me."

Abruptly Mrs. Merriweather sobered and her expression took on a grave look. "Yes, there is that," she said. "And ordinarily perhaps I should say the same. But a man has died. A man with an extraordinarily strong connection to your family, from the resemblance of his countenance to your father's. And when death has come in such a way to a household, there can be no more secrets. Though I should have a care, just now, what I asked of whom, my dear."

"That's just it!" Pamela exclaimed. "I feel as if I daren't ask anything of anyone."

Mrs. Merriweather nodded. "Tell me," she said in a gentle voice, "all about your family."

"What is there to tell?"

"How does your aunt come to live here? And your cousins?"

"Aunt Gwendolyn is my grandfather, Lord Kendall's, sister. When her husband, Mr. Avery, left her all but penniless, my grandparents invited them to come and live at Kendall Hall. My cousins have lived here for as long as I can remember."

"Tell me about your cousins."

Pamela frowned. She hesitated. Mrs. Merriweather smiled but it was not a smile of amusement. Instead she said, in a worrisome voice, "I wish very much to help your mother. But I cannot if I do not know what might have led to this moment. I am discreet! Just ask your mother, if you doubt it. Also recollect that your mother must have known I would ask you such questions and she still felt you should spend time with me."

And suddenly Pamela knew Mrs. Merriweather was quite right. Mama had asked her to spend the day with the woman not just because she was concerned about her safety, though no doubt she was, but precisely because she hoped Mrs. Merriweather would glean from Pamela what Mama could not bring herself to tell. It was just the sort of thing Mama would do. Pamela was not pleased but she took a deep breath and began to speak.

"They say Richard used to spend almost all his time in London. So much as he could afford to do so upon the allowance my grandfather made him. But then there was some trouble and he went to London less often. Only in the past year or so has he begun to revert to his old ways. As for my cousin Daphne, no one has ever told me the precise story but I collect she made a brilliant come-out in London. They say there were many gentlemen who wished to marry her. And she refused them all. She came home from her third Season and refused to leave Kendall Hall after that. No one has ever told me why and I cannot find the courage to ask her. Indeed, I should think no one can."

"Tell me about your uncle," Mrs. Merriweather said.

Pamela started. "M-m-my uncle?" she stammered.

"Yes, your father's twin brother," Mrs. Merriweather persisted.

Pamela took a moment to collect her thoughts. She had heard so many stories herself it took time to sift through them all and reduce them to those few facts of which she was certain.

"Papa's twin brother, older by some twenty minutes, was a wastrel. The scandal of the family. He was killed in a duel when I was still a baby. There can be no mistake for there were any number of witnesses. And yet, I must wonder, since this dead man looked so much like Father, whether my uncle did not perhaps survive all these years and finally decided to come back home."

"Which would have deprived your father of his rank and prospects," Mrs. Merriweather said thoughtfully.

Instantly Pamela was on her feet facing the former governess. Her hands were clenched into fists at her side. "You are not to say so! Papa would never have hurt his own brother! How dare you suggest such a thing?"

"I did not suggest it," Mrs. Merriweather said mildly. "I merely commented on his situation. But if you hear it as an accusation, then you may well suppose others will presume it to be the truth."

"But if it was my uncle, somehow still alive, why did he never let us know he was alive? And why choose to come back now?" Pamela whispered. "Why come back and terrify us all?" She paused as a thought occurred to her. "I wonder if this dead man, my uncle or not, was here the night of the ball. If it was he who spoke to everyone so oddly. For we were all upset the next day and you yourself heard all the speculation over the apparent oddity of my father's behavior."

Mrs. Merriweather nodded. "I agree. I, too, judge it to be almost certain that the dead man, whoever he may be, attended the ball and played the part of your father. The better to stir up trouble, I must suppose. I presume your uncle *was* a man who liked to stir up trouble?"

"Every chance he could, that much I have always heard," Pamela said, reaching back into her memory. "They say that every time he was home, there was shouting and fighting. I am told that even the servants used to shiver and hide when he was home."

"So no one was sorry to hear of his death," Mrs. Merriweather said thoughtfully. "And no one would have been happy to hear he was alive."

"Except Grandmama. She always loved Harry. She has his portrait in her sitting room and stares at it all the time," Pamela said diffidently.

Mrs. Merriweather nodded. "She was, after all, his mother."

They were both silent for several long moments. Then Pamela looked at Mrs. Merriweather. There was a troubled expression upon her face but she could think of no way to erase it. Not after this conversation.

"If it was my uncle, they will think Papa did it, won't they? To protect his position?"

The moment she had spoken, Pamela wished she could recall the words. But it was too late. Mrs. Merriweather looked at her with a most sympathetic gaze and that hurt worse than anything she could have said.

Julian was, to put the matter charitably, rather distracted as he rode toward home. Perhaps that was why he did not see the man until he was almost upon him.

The fellow had a disreputable look and an air of having lived in foreign parts. For one thing, he did not show the slightest deference to Julian that would have been expected of a peasant toward a young gentleman.

The man reached out and grasped Julian's bridle. " 'Ere now, was you up to the 'all?" he demanded in a rough voice that carried a hint of an accent Julian could not place.

"What is it to you where I have been?"

The man had the audacity to laugh and Julian pulled his bridle free of the man's grasp. Now Julian's voice was icy as he repeated his question. "Why should you care where I have been?"

"Oi don't," the man replied with an impudent grin. "Oi wants to know about a certain gen'lemun wot went up there yestermorn."

Julian drew in his breath with an audible hiss. Instantly the man moved closer. "You've seen 'im then? Wot's 'appening there? Somat an uproar, oi'll be bound."

"Oh, an uproar indeed," Julian agreed, trying to collect his stunned wits. "Would you like to go and see for yourself?"

"No, no!" the man said fervently, backing a few steps away. " 'E said to wait and oi'll waits."

"I see." Julian drew in another deep breath, beginning to feel a trifle more in control. "Well, then, what did you hope I could tell you?"

" 'Ow is they taking it? 'Is reappearance, oi means? 'E said they wouldn't loike it none. Said they'd be stunned loike when 'e appeared."

"Oh, they were stunned all right," Julian agreed. "And I think it safe to say they did not like it."

The man cackled his laughter so loudly that Julian's mount began to prance sideways, startled by the sound. Julian quieted him, and tried to discover what he could.

"If you will not go up to the hall, would you like

to come down to the tavern in town? I should be happy to buy you a drink."

"Why?" the man asked, his suspicion instantly apparent.

Julian shrugged and raised his eyebrows. "Oh, in hopes of gaining information about yon sudden appearance," he said, as though sharing a jest with the man. "Anyone who can discompose the earl and his family so thoroughly is worth knowing about. I've not seen anyone accomplish what your friend has in so short a time."

The man hesitated, then shook his head. "No. 'E said oi weren't to talk to no'un. 'E'd be angry to know oi've talked wif you. But oi 'ad to know."

"Of course you did," Julian agreed, trying frantically to think of a way to keep the man by his side until the constable could be found.

If this stranger had talked with no one, that would explain why he did not know that his friend was dead. For Julian was certain the man's friend was the dead man. It was the only probable explanation.

So now Julian exerted himself to be charming. He leaned toward the man. "If you like, I should be glad to meet you here again later. Or tomorrow. And tell you of any news I can discover."

The man hesitated, then nodded. "Same time tomorrer," he said, then faded back into the trees by the side of the road.

Julian stared after him, bemused, for several moments as he tried to decide whether he should ride back to the hall to warn them. In the end he decided that since the man was no doubt watching him, it would not be wise. So instead he slowly made the rest of his way home.

He had not quite reached his ancestral home, however, when he saw a familiar carriage traveling in the opposite direction. Julian pulled up and signaled to the carriage to stop.

"Hallo, young Deerwood. What is it, m'boy?" Sir Geoffrey asked.

Julian told him about the stranger who had accosted him.

"Thank you, m'boy. I am on my way to the hall now and shall see what I can discover."

Julian watched with very mixed feelings as the magistrate's carriage rattled along. He only hoped he had not made matters worse for Pamela. But he did not see what else he could have done. Someone had murdered a man at the hall, and until that person was found out, he could not be sure Pamela herself was not in danger. And this was the only way he could think of to protect her if she would not leave the hall and come to his parents' home.

With that thought to console himself, Julian continued on his way home.

Chapter 14

Pamela looked out of her bedroom window. It was a warm night and she could not bear to be trapped behind the heavy curtains. Not when so much troubled her thoughts.

As she watched, a figure slipped through the shrubbery. She leaned forward to try to discover who it might be. And then she saw a second one. The first was a woman, the second a man. And from the way they embraced, she would say they were lovers. Or so she supposed, for Pamela had to admit she had no knowledge of such things save what she read in novels and Mama was forever telling her they were rubbish.

But when two people ran toward one another and embraced, what else was one to think? Her only consolation was that the man was not Julian. Even from this distance, even in the dark, she was sure that in her heart she would have known had it been him. But then who was the man? And who the woman?

For a moment Pamela was tempted to slip out of her room and downstairs to find out. But that would have been foolish. By the time she could have dressed and reached the ground floor, they would be gone. Already they were heading for the maze. And Pamela had no doubt they meant to lose themselves there, safe from prying eyes such as her own.

Still, she felt she ought to do something! Ought she to watch for them to return? But what if they went around to the other side of the house? Ought she to wake her parents and tell them? But what if one of them was of the pair? Pamela knew that of late there had been a discord between them and she knew not the reason. But something of the sort that she had seen might well account for it.

In the end, Pamela did something she could not have imagined herself doing just a short week before. She went in search of the former governess, Mrs. Merriweather, to ask for her assistance. It seemed, after all, the most sensible thing to be done.

Mrs. Merriweather had retired for the night but she answered her door in such short order that Pamela could be certain she need not, at least, reproach herself for waking the poor woman. And indeed she held a book in her hand, signaling what her occupation had been. Behind her stood her maid who clutched a candlestick as though prepared to defend her mistress with it, if need be.

At the sight of Pamela's face, Mrs. Merriweather drew the girl inside her room and carefully, silently shut the door behind them. She indicated to her maid that the poor woman should set the candlestick down. "For Miss Fairchild poses no threat to me, I assure you," Mrs. Merriweather said. Then she asked the girl gently, "What has happened, my dear?"

Pamela looked at the maid and hesitated. "I shan't say a word to anyone about anything, not without Mrs. Merriweather tells me to," that woman said stoutly.

"Take a deep breath and tell me," the former governess advised kindly. "Neither Kate nor I shall tell anyone."

So Pamela told Mrs. Merriweather what she had seen. And her fears. She also told her why she had not simply waited up for their return.

"Quite right," the older woman said approvingly. "And quite right to come to me. I do not think it likely either of your parents were below for Lady Fairchild left my room and I heard her talking in the hallway with your father just a few moments before you knocked. But I mislike the encounter nonetheless. At a time such as this, so soon after a man's violent death yesterday morning and the attack upon me last night, one would think everyone would choose to stay indoors and safely in their rooms."

Pamela wished she dared ask what her mother had been talking with Mrs. Merriweather about. But she did not. Instead she hesitantly said, "I am told that lovers are often indiscreet and do not think of what may or may not be sensible."

Mrs. Merriweather laughed, but before Pamela could take offense, the former governess demanded, "What do you know of lovers, my dear?"

"I have read things," she answered stiffly.

The older woman put her hand over Pamela's. "I am sure you have," she said. "And you may be right that that is all that is going on. But I am of a particularly suspicious turn of mind, you see. And for me, I must wonder if perhaps there is more to it than that. I think perhaps I shall go for a midnight stroll."

Instantly Pamela felt alarmed. "But you must not!" she protested. "What if you should be right? Then might there not be danger? Mama would never forgive me for placing you in its way."

"That's right! You ought not to go out there," the maid said sternly, moving to stand between her mistress and the door.

But Mrs. Merriweather was not to be deterred. "This time I am prepared."

From her reticule, which to be sure was rather larger than one might call fashionable, she withdrew a small pistol. It was cunningly made and Mrs. Merriweather smiled with grim satisfaction.

"I daresay I shall be safe from danger tonight. A good thing my dear husband, Colonel Merriweather, insisted that I travel with this, in the event of highwaymen. Kate, help me dress."

Grumbling the entire time, the maid helped Mrs. Merriweather don a gown over her nightshift.

As Pamela watched, she said uneasily, "Perhaps I ought to come with you, Mrs. Merriweather. I am persuaded that Mama would say that I should."

But the former governess shook her head. "I may be able to claim an eccentricity that causes me to wander about late at night but you could not. For your family would know it was not your habit. No, my dear, wait here for me with Kate and I shall tell you everything when I return."

With some misgivings, Pamela watched the woman go. It went against the grain to let her do so, but she could think of no way to stop her and her words seemed sensible. So she sat down to wait. Because she had nothing else to do and Kate seemed disinclined to talk, she picked up the book Mrs. Merriweather had set aside and began to read.

Downstairs, Mrs. Merriweather shivered. She was not quite so sanguine about her safety as she had told the girl. But there was no choice. She had to find out what was going on and she could not take the chance of putting Pamela or Kate at risk by letting them come along.

Outside she shivered yet again. It was a warm night but Mrs. Merriweather felt a chill go through her nonetheless. She took a deep breath and moved in the direction Pamela had seen the wayward couple venture. She had not gone far when she saw someone else. To her shock, it was Lady Gwendolyn. She was alone, and try as she could, Mrs. Merriweather could see no one else nearby. In any event, the thought that this older, pinch-faced woman might have undertaken a clandestine meeting with a man seemed wildly implausible.

Lady Gwendolyn started at the sight of the former governess. "My dear Mrs. Merriweather!" she exclaimed. "What are you doing out here at this time of night?"

That was precisely the question Mrs. Merriweather wished she could ask, but instead she tried to look vague as she waved a hand about and said, "I could not resist taking a turn in the fresh air before I retired. It will help me sleep, you know."

"I see. But do you think it entirely wise? Particularly after your misadventure of last night?"

Mrs. Merriweather forced herself to titter in that mindless way she could not abide. "Oh, but surely that housebreaker is long gone by now? And who would attack me twice?"

Lady Gwendolyn looked as though she wished she could dump a bucket of cold water over the other woman's head and Mrs. Merriweather had to admit that in her place she would feel precisely the same. Lady Gwendolyn settled for regarding her with an expression of cold dislike and swept past her toward the hall.

Mrs. Merriweather watched her go and then continued in the direction from which Lady Gwendolyn had come. It seemed impossible that she could be the woman Pamela had seen. Which meant that the couple was still to be found. So she pressed on, perhaps a trifle too precipitously, for the next thing she knew, she had stepped in what must have been a rabbit hole and fell down.

Cautiously Mrs. Merriweather felt her ankle but it seemed she had the good fortune not to have twisted it. As she sat there, making certain, she heard a sound and became very still. Now she blessed rather than cursed the carelessness that had resulted in her fall. Two voices carried in the quiet of the night. Mrs. Merriweather had, it seemed, found her couple.

A moment later she realized her mistake. It was not a man and a woman she heard, but rather two men. One of them seemed crude but the other spoke in cultured accents she recognized only too well and her heart sank. Here was trouble indeed if Lord Fairchild was meeting in secret with villains.

And then, as though that were not enough, she did hear the couple. A woman laughed softly and a man hushed her. But the voices were young and Mrs. Merriweather supposed she could guess to whom they belonged. Really, she thought with some asperity, who would have thought that the grounds of an earl's estate would be so crowded at such an unseemly hour of the night?

The two parties must have heard one another for abruptly all voices ceased talking. There came the sounds of footsteps running away and others creeping more stealthily toward the house. Mrs. Merriweather sighed. Now that they had heard one another, everyone would be very careful to stay out of sight. She might as well go back inside the house herself, she thought, for it was most unlikely that she would learn anything to the point after this.

With the same care for stealth as the others, Mrs. Merriweather made her way back inside the hall and up the main stairs, for she reasoned those were the stairs the others were least likely to use. As a result of not having to detour as the others did, the former governess reached her door well before anyone else. And she was waiting just outside it when the first person appeared, slipping unseen, or so the woman patently thought, out of the panel that hid the servants' door on this floor.

It was not, however, anyone Mrs. Merriweather had expected. Instead, she found herself face to face with Daphne Avery. Both women blinked at the sight of the other.

Daphne apparently decided to brazen matters out for she said carelessly, "Mrs. Merriweather, you are up very late! Do you have trouble sleeping?"

"No more than you, my dear," was the placid reply.

And then, because she knew Daphne's voice must have warned anyone else hiding on the servants' stairs, Mrs. Merriweather smiled and retreated into her room. There Pamela rose to her feet at once and came toward her, as did Kate.

"Well? Did you see them? Did you see who they were?" Pamela demanded.

Mrs. Merriweather shook her head. At the sight of the girl's disappointed expression, however, she smiled and said, "Never mind. I learned a great deal that might or might not be useful. Including the fact that your entire family seems prone to wander about at the oddest hours."

"Perhaps they were looking for the couple as well?" the girl suggested hopefully.

"Perhaps."

A few more soothing words and it was possible to send Miss Fairchild back to her room. Kate was not so easily satisfied. "Trouble, Mrs. Merriweather. That's what you're asking for, going out this time of night and poking into other people's business. Won't like it, they won't."

"Yes, but it had to be done," Mrs. Merriweather replied soothingly.

"Not by you," her maid retorted bluntly. "Ought to sleep in here tonight, I ought. Just in case any of 'em takes a notion to harm you again."

Eventually, however, Mrs. Merriweather managed to send Kate off to bed, assuring her that she would be safe enough with her door locked. Once alone, however, she lay awake for some time, pondering what she had seen and what she had overheard. None of it made any sense but all of it troubled her. With a man two days dead, how could it not?

Eventually, common sense asserted itself and Mrs. Merriweather blew out her candle and forced herself to go to sleep. Perhaps, she thought, she ought to send for Andrew. She could not abandon Lady Fairchild when her former charge's affairs were in such disorder, but perhaps it would be as well to have the colonel close at hand. He might see something she did not.

And so, with that comforting thought, Marian fell into a dreaming sleep and never even noticed when someone turned a key in the lock from outside the room and her door briefly opened and then as quickly closed again.

Chapter 15

It was the body in the lane that did it. The second body to be found on the Earl of Kendall's land that caused such an uproar. Particularly when it was Julian Deerwood who was called upon to identify the poor creature. He, it seemed, was the only person who would own to having ever seen the man before.

This was not a circumstance likely to endear him to the Kendall household and briefly it seemed as if they might decide to ban him from the hall. But somehow Pamela managed to persuade them otherwise.

"We have known him all these years!" she protested. "Surely none of you truly believe him capable of wishing us harm? Or of trying to cause it? Is it his fault that he happened upon the man yesterday? He told Sir Geoffrey at once that it was so."

"If he is telling the truth," Richard said with a mischievous grin.

Pamela rounded on her cousin, ready to ring a peal over his head but there was no need. Lord Fairchild sighed and said, "Yes, yes, we know that Julian Deerwood has our best interests at heart. But something must be done about these happenings. Two murders within the space of a week! It is not to be borne."

It was his wife who, staring at him oddly, said, "And how do you propose to prevent it, Edward? I cannot think these murders will stop simply because they meet with our disapproval."

Lady Winley rose to her feet. "Well I, for one, mean

to tolerate this no longer. Come, Catherine, we leave today for London. I shall not have you tainted by this scandal."

"I am afraid, Lady Winley, that I must ask you to stay a little longer," a voice said from the doorway.

They all turned to see Sir Geoffrey standing there and he advanced into the room. He bowed and smiled a perfunctory smile. "I am sorry," he said gravely, "but I must ask that no one leave. Not until I am closer to a solution to these two mysteries."

"But they can have nothing to do with us!" Lady Winley protested.

Sir Geoffrey bowed again. "Perhaps not," he said, as gravely as before, "but they did not occur until you arrived in the neighborhood!"

Not one person in the room thought Sir Geoffrey truly suspected Lady Winley of a connection to the murders but not one felt other than a strong desire to cheer at the setdown he had just given her. As for the lady herself, she gripped the back of the nearest chair and pressed a hand to her chest. She opened and closed her mouth several times as though she wished to speak but could think of nothing to say. Her color went from red to pale to red again and finally she turned her back on the magistrate.

He merely smiled and turned to Mrs. Merriweather. "Will you come with me?" he asked.

"Yes, of course," she replied. She paused, however, to speak to the earl. She held out a letter. "Would you frank this for me, sir? It is a message to my husband, Colonel Merriweather. I should not wish him to worry if gossip should have reached so far."

"Certainly, Mrs. Merriweather."

And then, with a reassuring smile for Lady Fairchild and an innate dignity that surpassed even that of the countess, the former governess followed the magistrate from the drawing room and into the parlor he had used the other times he had questioned members of the family. With a greater solicitude than he had thus far shown anyone else, he handed her to a seat and bowed.

"I am sorry to put you to such inconvenience and perhaps add to your natural distress but I can think of no one else in this house whose understanding is so superior."

"Nor who is so detached from the circumstances?"

He indicated the justice of her words by another bow. She nodded. "In your place I should feel just the same," the former governess acknowledged. "What is it you wish to ask of me?"

He hesitated and took a turn or two about the room before he answered her. "How great a loyalty do you feel to this household?"

Mrs. Merriweather placed her hands in her lap and chose her words with great care. "I value justice, sir. I would not shield a murderer. But neither would I gossip about anyone unless I knew it to be relevant to the case at hand."

Sir Geoffrey nodded. "They will have heard, I presume, about the latest body?"

"Of a certainty. It is all they can speak of. But perhaps this does suggest a common murderer? Someone not of this household?" Mrs. Merriweather ventured to ask. "For surely there can be no question this latest person was murdered outside the hall?"

Sir Geoffrey did not bother to answer her directly. Instead he said, "I commend your loyalty but require your intelligence, Mrs. Merriweather."

"How?"

He told her.

Julian met Pamela in the garden. He looked shaken and she immediately went to him. He held her close. When they finally stepped away from each other, she tried to collect her wits. She spoke before he could do so.

"Miss Winley is troubled, of course, but bearing up well, I should say," Pamela told him, rushing her words. "Her mother wishes to remove her but Sir Geoffrey has told her that is not yet possible. So you still have time to fix your interest with her."

"I don't wish to fix my interest with her!"

Pamela looked at him, at the dismay on his face, and shook her head. "You are saying so because you have had a fight with her. But there is still time to patch it up."

He ceased to argue then and she knew she had the right of it. But oh, how she wished she were wrong!

Julian stared at his childhood friend. How much he wished he could make things all better for her, take away this horror hanging over her head, remove the threat to her family. But he could not. He could not even pretend not to care about Miss Winley, for Pamela knew him too well. He felt at a severe loss as to what to say.

"Do you know who he was?" Pamela asked him.

Julian hesitated. It was not precisely that Sir Geoffrey had asked him not to tell, but he knew that was what the magistrate would have preferred. Still, this was Pamela, his childhood friend.

"I believe the man to have known the other man who died. He did not know that his friend had been killed, at least not yesterday when he spoke to me. But he knew that the fellow's appearance would cause an uproar. Pamela, I have been thinking and I wonder if it could have been your uncle. The one who ought to have inherited your grandfather's title. I know that everyone says he died years ago but I wonder. Because the man who spoke to me expected the other's appearance to cause a great uproar. And why else would it matter enough to murder a man?"

She took a moment to pace about with great agitation. But when Julian would have gone to her, she held out a hand to ward him off.

"No, I must think," she said. "My uncle. It seems impossible. There were witnesses to his death. And yet, I confess my own thoughts have run the same course as yours. I do agree that if you are right it would explain a great deal. But Julian," she said, as though trying to persuade both her friend and herself, "why would my uncle come back now? Why would he never have let anyone know he was alive? No, surely it cannot be. Not when there were so many people who saw him die."

"Perhaps they were mistaken? And perhaps he did let someone know he was still alive," Julian replied. "Perhaps that person kept silent. Until your uncle returned and then that person did away with him entirely."

Pamela hesitated. She believed it likely, but she didn't want to do so. The pallor of her face proved that. Indeed she went so pale that in two strides he was beside her, sliding an arm around her waist to help hold her up and cursing himself for his folly in speaking so freely.

"Come. Sit down over here," Julian said. "This is all very shocking, I know. And I wish I might be wrong. Perhaps I am. There is no proof, after all, that my suppositions are correct."

"There is no proof against them, either," she said bravely. "I wonder if we should tell Sir Geoffrey what we suspect?"

Julian shook his head. "There is no need. I do not doubt, from the tenor of his questions, that the same notion has already occurred to him. I presume he is already looking into the possibility."

He paused and took her hands in his. "I will not let you suffer, no matter what the truth may be. I will take you away from here, if need be, and protect you from anyone who would dare to speak against you."

But instead of feeling pleased, instead of looking up to him with gratitude, Pamela pulled her hands free.

Her voice became distinctly cold as she replied, "Miss Winley might not care for that."

He made a dismissive gesture with his hand. "Miss Winley has nothing to say to the matter. I shall do what I think right."

"And subject me to all the more gossip because of it!" she retorted tartly. She even, he realized with a start, had given a sigh of exasperation. "Do you not think anything through, Julian?"

He rose to his feet, offended. "I was trying to help," he said with stiff dignity. At least he hoped it sounded like dignity. "I meant to offer you my protection. But if you do not wish for it, if my good wishes mean nothing to you, then there is no more to be said."

Whatever he expected, it was not for Pamela to begin to laugh at him. Now it was Julian who was exasperated. "Dash it all, Pamela! You can't laugh at a fellow who is trying to help you! You really can't."

She held out a hand in apology. "I am sorry, Julian. It is just that it seems I must either laugh or cry," she said. "It seems there is no way out of this trouble and wild schemes will not help."

"Then marry me."

For a long moment, the two stared at each other in appalled, stunned silence. Then Pamela whirled around and fled from him, fled toward the house. Julian watched her go, his mouth hanging open. Well, if that wasn't the most unflattering reaction to a fellow's marriage proposal! And he had thought Pamela liked him.

There was no accounting for women, he told himself. No accounting at all.

Lady Gwendolyn Avery was not a clever woman. If she had been, she would never have married Mr. Avery. But she was tenacious and fiercely protective of her children. She did not, could not, ever regret the death of her nephew Harry, the late Lord Fairchild.

She had not questioned the news of his death at the

time of the duel. She had not, she realized, wanted to question it. She had been too relieved to have him gone from their lives. But now, as she listened to Pamela and Mr. Deerwood talking, from her sheltered spot behind a hedge, Lady Gwendolyn felt as though she had been struck.

Harry? Her nephew alive all these years? Could it be true? Could someone have known and kept it secret? She felt foolish that she had been so fierce in her denials, even to herself, of that possibility.

Lady Gwendolyn thought back to the night of the ball. To Daphne's behavior. And Richard's. Had they spoken to their cousin Harry? It would account for the change in their manner since that night. But why, then, had they not confided in her? After the man was found dead, if not before?

To be sure, it was still all speculation. And she did not want to believe Harry had been alive until such a short time before. Better to continue her denials, both to herself and others. Except that if he had lived through that duel and someone had known, that fact might be turned to her advantage, if she could only see how.

With a grim determination to discover the truth, Lady Gwendolyn turned to head back toward the house. She did not know what she would do if Daphne or Richard confirmed Pamela and young Deerwood's suspicions. But she had to know. Later she could decide what she would do.

One other thing she intended, however. If it was possible, Lady Gwendolyn did not wish anyone outside the family to discover the truth of the matter. There had been far too much scandal already and she would do anything to prevent more. That, however, was something the person who killed Harry, if it was Harry and if she could discover who had done so, need never know.

She stopped abruptly. Pamela had fled to the house,

leaving young Deerwood just standing there. Perhaps it would be as well to drop a hint in his ear? To warn him away from Pamela? Then his thoughts might become focused on that, rather than on unraveling family secrets he had no business to be thinking about.

Lady Gwendolyn straightened her shoulders and stepped forward, toward Deerwood.

Julian felt a strong sense of injury. So much so that he did not even notice the woman watching him. Not until she spoke to him, at any rate.

"So you want to marry Pamela? You are a fool to think she will have you! Or that my brother, the earl, will ever allow such a thing. A mere baron's son for his precious granddaughter? It is not to be thought of!"

"Lady Gwendolyn!"

The woman strolled closer. She shook her head. "All the same, you young people. Far too impetuous. Kindhearted, I will give you that, but too impetuous. You had as well cast your eyes on the visitor from London, Miss Winley, as on Pamela."

Julian flushed at these words. He could hear the malice in her voice and he had no doubt that Lady Gwendolyn had noted his interest in Catherine and was now turning it against him. But what was he to say?

She apparently tired of the game for she half turned away and her voice was impatient as she said, "Oh, go away. You are far too easy to bait."

Julian found he felt more sorry for her than angry. Indeed, he took a step toward her without thinking through what he meant to do.

"Lady Gwendolyn," he said, "I know that all of you must be very distressed. And with good reason. If there is anything I can do to help any of you, please tell me."

She stared at him and he could see the distress in

her eyes that had not been apparent at a distance. But she did not speak. Perhaps she thought him too young to be of any help; perhaps she thought him impertinent to ask. In any event, Lady Gwendolyn shook her head and then fled for the house just as Pamela had done such a short time before.

Julian watched her go, bewildered. "You've a poor touch with the ladies of late," he told himself.

"That you do!" a voice said from behind him.

Julian groaned and turned to see who was taunting him now. "Avery!" he said with some exasperation. "I suppose you have come to mock me as well?"

The other man strolled forward. He was dressed, as always, in outmoded elegance. "I? No, I've better things to do with my time than taunt a fellow sufferer. You are not the first person ever to be disappointed in love, you know," he said.

Julian latched on to two words. "Fellow sufferer?" he echoed doubtfully for he could not recall Avery ever showing a serious interest in any young lady.

Richard Avery waved a hand. "Never mind. It is the brandy speaking. I have been indulging, you see, even if it is ridiculously early in the day," he confided and only then did Julian realize how drunk the other was. Avery went on, "What else is one to do when dead bodies keep turning up? And when one's family seems inevitably about to be plunged into scandal?"

"One might make a push to resolve the mystery," Julian heard himself say.

"Me?" Avery laughed and it was not a pleasant sound. "My family would no doubt lock me up if they thought I was prying into their secrets! No, I thank you, I will leave that task to the magistrate and his assistants, whomever they might be. Me, I shall continue to drink. As heavily as I can manage. Until this is all over. And then, why then I might put a bullet through my brain."

At these words, Richard lurched forward and Julian

moved to catch and hold him as he was violently ill. Somehow he felt much older than the other young man even though the reality was the reverse.

"You cannot continue to do this," Julian scolded. "Your family has need of you."

When he could answer, Richard's words were harsh. "Me? No, they have no need of me. They think me a wastrel and I am. I am no use to anyone. Indeed, I think I have failed everyone who has ever needed me."

And then, before Julian could argue with him further, Richard wrenched himself free and stumbled off farther away from the house. Julian dropped onto the nearest bench. He felt as though he had wandered into Bedlam and never even noticed. But surely, for the moment, he was guaranteed some peace?

He was mistaken. Only moments later Miss Winley came into sight. She was dressed as fetchingly as he had ever seen her, and for a moment, Julian forgot that he had proposed to Pamela.

"Catherine!" Then, at her icy expression, he said, abashedly, "That is to say, Miss Winley."

She halted, taken aback at the sight of him. Then she seemed to recover. She came forward, smiled, and held out her hand to him. "Mr. Deerwood! You are very kind to visit us when I vow the rest of the neighborhood avoids Kendall Hall as though we had the plague here."

Julian flushed but took her hand and drew her to sit on the bench beside him. "How are you doing?" he asked. "It must be most unpleasant for you to be in the midst of all of this."

"It is!" she agreed fervently. "When Miss Fairchild wrote to invite me, she promised parties and picnics and other entertainments, and instead we only sit inside with everyone presenting the dourest of faces. Or we can walk about the grounds. But that is all. I do not think she recalls our presence, Mama's and mine, and certainly she takes no care for our entertainment."

Julian blinked. He stared at the beautiful vision before him. Carefully he chose his words. "You would not wish Pamela to be thinking of games and parties when her family is in such distress, surely?"

"Why not? It is not as though there is anything she can do to help them. Or to alter matters. So why shouldn't she think of her guests? Why shouldn't she think of games and parties and such?"

Julian could only shake his head. "You do not understand her sensibilities."

"Well, she does not understand mine!"

And with that, Catherine Winley rose to her feet and marched away. Too late Julian thought to warn her about Richard. But even drunk as he was, it was not likely he would offer her any insult and the worst that might occur was that she would observe him being unpleasantly ill. And if so, Julian could not help thinking, it would only serve her as she deserved.

So he did not follow or try to call her back. Instead he took a deep breath and headed into the hall. He had to speak to Pamela before he left, no matter how reluctant she might be. Someone must protect her from the madness here and he could not see who else it might be if it were not him.

Chapter 16

Pamela would have liked to talk to Mrs. Merriweather. But when she reached the house, the woman was nowhere to be found. When she ventured to ask her grandmother, Lady Kendall sniffed and replied, "She is with your mother, though what they can have in common to talk about I cannot think! Nor why your mother should trust her, though I suppose she may find some comfort in her company. Still, I do not approve of nor do I trust the woman. I understand Mrs. Merriweather to have been closeted with Sir Geoffrey for some time this morning. To what purpose I cannot imagine. She is a stranger here, your mother's onetime governess. What can she know of this business?"

"As much as anyone, I should suppose," Pamela could not help but retort.

Now Lady Kendall looked directly at her, a very odd expression on her face. For a moment Pamela almost reached out to her, so alarmed was she by her grandmother's expression. But then Lady Kendall recovered herself and imperiously waved Pamela away.

"You know nothing at all about this," Lady Kendall said. "And I devoutly pray that you are mistaken in Mrs. Merriweather and that neither does she."

And then Lady Kendall swept past Pamela and, like the rest of her family, out of her sight. The younger woman felt shaken for she could not ever recall seeing her grandmother behave in such a way. Always before she seemed to have perfect command over herself, her voice, her emotions.

Without quite understanding the impulse within her, Pamela decided to seek refuge in the nursery. She told herself that it was because she liked her youngest brother and that she was curious to see Mrs. Merriweather's child. Underneath it all, however, was the knowledge that in Nurse, at least, she was confident of finding a sympathetic ear.

She paused in the doorway of the nursery, suddenly reluctant to disturb her brother at his studies. Or the delightful picture of the little girl who was playing with Nurse. Almost she retreated. But then Nurse looked up and saw her and beckoned Pamela into the nursery. Her brother looked up from his studies, flung down his pen, and ran to hug. Once again she felt safe, once again she felt as if everything would be all right.

"Well, well, Miss Fairchild! It has been some time since you favored us with a visit," Nurse said in a severe tone belied by the smile on her face and the humor in her eyes. "As if you could not be done with us fast enough once you outgrew the schoolroom."

Pamela smiled in return and hugged first her brother and then her old nurse. "I have neglected you and I am sorry for it."

But Nurse would have none of it. "Nonsense! You're a young lady now and you've other things to worry about than us. Especially in the past few days," she added soberly.

Both smiles faltered. Her younger brother asked cheerfully, "Why in the past few days?"

"He doesn't know?" Pamela asked Nurse.

The older woman shook her head. "We've done our best to shield him from it. And will continue to do so for as long as possible."

"Good."

"Mmm. Why don't we go into my room and have a chat about it all?" Nurse suggested.

But by now the little girl had noticed that everyone was surrounding Pamela and she demanded attention from her too. Pamela picked her up and said, "Is this Mrs. Merriweather's daughter?"

Nurse's expression hardened. "Yes. A dear little creature. But her mother simply does not understand how a well-ordered nursery should be run. I shudder to think what conditions must exist for the tyke at home."

Pamela made no comment, recognizing at once that her old nurse's dislike must have sprung from a challenge to her authority. Dearly as she loved the woman, she knew her to be jealous of her control over the nursery and unwilling to brook the slightest interference. But Pamela found herself thinking that if she were a mother, she would want to be able to visit her children in the nursery whenever she wished.

"What will the children do while we talk?" Pamela asked, trying to turn Nurse's attention away from her evident grievance.

"Elizabeth will play at our feet with whatever toy we give her, for she's a sweet, biddable child, and we may talk freely for she is much too young to understand or remember anything we might say. And your brother will continue working on his lessons, just as he ought."

As this was said with a minatory look at the boy, he promptly sat back down at the table and began to work again on his book. With a nod of satisfaction, Nurse led Pamela back to her little room. There she indicated that the young lady should take a seat in the straight-back chair while she reposed in the rocker.

"Now," Nurse said briskly, once they were settled, "tell me what is going on. With the family. With all these dead bodies that have been turning up. With yourself that you must come to me for counsel."

Pamela did so, feeling a great sense of relief as she unburdened herself. Unfortunately, the more she said, the more distressed Nurse became until it was patent to Pamela that she would find no comfort here. No easy assurances that all would be well. No, Nurse was far too upset for that. In the end, Pamela told her everything except the suspicion she and Julian had that the first man who had died was her uncle. She could not bring herself to put that into words.

But perhaps she didn't need to do so. From a word here or there that Nurse let drop, Pamela realized the woman already knew a great deal about the family's affairs. Clearly far more than Pamela did herself. The thought rankled. But then, Nurse had been around far longer than Pamela. Perhaps in time she would know just as much. The question was, would she want to know?

She had just finished telling Nurse about Julian's proposal when they both realized they were not alone. Pamela looked up to see Mrs. Merriweather standing in the doorway of Nurse's room. She did not look pleased. Indeed, the moment Pamela noticed her, the woman moved forward and scooped up her daughter.

"I cannot believe you let Elizabeth play on the floor like this, so near the dirty fireplace!" Mrs. Merriweather said indignantly. "Or that you do not think to stop her from putting things in her mouth."

Nurse rose to her feet. Pamela recognized the stormy expression on her face and would have moved back had it been possible. But there was nowhere to go. So she tried to stay quiet and out of their way.

"I have been taking care of babies for these thirty years and more. I'll thank you not to say I don't know how!" Nurse began. "You mothers think you know everything, but you don't! I'd not put any child in danger and well you should know it."

Mrs. Merriweather opened her mouth to give a countercharge but at that precise moment the baby began to wail and she had her hands full trying to calm the child. She could not. It only added insult to everything else, however, that the moment Nurse took the little girl, she quieted down and put her head against the woman.

Nurse regarded Mrs. Merriweather over the top of the child's head and smiled triumphantly. "There now, you see? The little one knows who is best suited to take care of her. They always do."

Mrs. Merriweather turned on her heel and stalked from the room muttering something that Pamela was just as glad she couldn't hear. Nurse was fussing over the child and reaching for a cloth to clean her face. Perhaps it would be just as well to slip away herself, Pamela decided.

In the hallway outside the nursery she found Mrs. Merriweather kicking the wall and still muttering to herself. Pamela might have been tempted to laugh had she not been feeling so overwhelmed.

The instant she saw her, Mrs. Merriweather stopped her odd behavior. She straightened, regarded Pamela sternly, and then her expression softened as she said, "Oh, my poor dear, you are even more overset than I am!"

And she was, of course. She simply didn't like to admit it nor wish to tell the story of Julian's proposal yet again. But Mrs. Merriweather had overheard more than Pamela supposed. Enough that she nodded to herself, and when she spoke, it was in a firm voice that would brook no opposition.

"Come. Let us go to my room and talk. I have had enough of this romantic nonsense between you and young Deerwood. It is most distracting and I wish to have it sorted out as soon as may be."

Pamela gaped at Mrs. Merriweather, but the woman seemed to be serious. Somehow it seemed impossible to refuse. So they went down the stairs and into the other woman's room. There, despite her natural reticence in speaking of such things to a stranger, Pamela found herself telling the story once again. Only this time, somehow more of her feelings crept into the tale. And her fears. When she was done, Mrs. Merriweather stared at her. She sighed.

"I am getting far too old for such nonsense. But I suppose I must not think in such a way for my own Elizabeth will go through just such things, I'll be bound. If only to vex me."

Pamela merely waited, warily, for whatever advice this strange woman might impart. But instead of dispensing advice, Mrs. Merriweather asked a question. "My dear, what are you afraid of?"

"Afraid?" Pamela echoed, taken aback. "Of what should I be afraid?"

Mrs. Merriweather merely regarded her steadily, and after a moment, Pamela sighed. "I am afraid he has given his heart to Miss Winley and I cannot bear the thought of being married to a man who cares for someone else."

"Particularly when you have already given your heart to him." Pamela started at this insight but Mrs. Merriweather ignored her and went on, "Yes, there is a great deal of wisdom in feeling as you do. One ought, however, to be certain the other person does care for someone else. Otherwise one might toss away what one would hold most dear."

"But I cannot be mistaken!"

"Oh?"

Pamela took another deep breath. "You do not understand. Julian told me himself how he feels about Miss Winley. He even asked me to invite her here even though I had not met her prior to her visit. I did so because we have always been friends and helped one another. But that is why he is asking me now. Because he wishes to help me out. But he cannot see what a torment it would be for me, knowing that he was thinking of her when he was with me."

Mrs. Merriweather took a turn or two about the small but comfortably furnished room. She stared hard at Pamela and then paced some more. Finally she spoke.

"I think perhaps it is you who does not understand. I have no doubt that Mr. Deerwood believed his affections to be engaged but I do not believe that he looks at Miss Winley as you think he does. As perhaps even he thinks he does. Not these past few days. Indeed, I should say that it is you he regards with a warmth I should want to see in any man who wished to marry my daughter."

Pamela opened her mouth to protest but Mrs. Merriweather held up a hand to forestall her. "No, do not tell me it is the affection of childhood playmates, for I should not believe you. Even if he does not yet know his own heart, Mr. Deerwood feels more for you than that. I do not say you should accept his suit. I cannot like such havey-cavey goings on. He ought to have spoken to your father first! But I do think you should allow him to spend time in your company. Look carefully to see if I am not right in this, about how he feels. Then make your decision."

Pamela stood, convinced that Mrs. Merriweather must be mistaken. But aloud she only said, "I could not refuse to see Julian anyway, not after all the years we have been friends. But I do not promise to listen to his suit. I am certain he only offered out of responsibility."

"Perhaps. But perhaps not. And do you know, Miss Fairchild, I have always thought that marriages which begin with friendship are the strongest ones of all?"

Pamela could stand it no longer. Every word cut through her, echoing as they did her dearest wishes.

"I must be going," she blurted out. "Mama will be looking for me. With all this nonsense about the dead men, she seems incapable of handling all those domestic details she was used to do without thinking. Now she depends upon my aid."

From the wry way that Mrs. Merriweather smiled

at her, Pamela had no doubt she understood the excuse for what it was. But she did not object. Indeed she waved Pamela out of the room amiably enough. But the words she had spoken would not go away and echoed in Pamela's mind as she went to find her mother.

Deerwood found Pamela coming down the main stairs just as he entered the main hall. She paused on the stairs at the sight of him and looked, for a moment, as if she meant to turn and go back up them.

"Wait! Please! Pamela, if I have upset you, I am so sorry. But please do not cut me off for that. Tell me, instead, what is wrong and let me make amends."

When she still hesitated, Julian added coaxingly, "Come, Pamela! Surely we have been friends too long to let it fall apart for want of any effort to sort things out."

At that, her expression softened and she came the rest of the way down until she stood right in front of him. He reached out and took her hand, scarcely conscious he did so. She looked up at him and all he wanted to do was hold her in a comforting embrace. He wanted to promise to protect her and keep her safe. But he dared not risk sending her flying away from him all over again.

And so, instead, Julian swallowed hard and said, as lightly as he could, though his voice still trembled, "I meant no hurt or offense, Pamela. Will you not tell me why my proposal was so offensive to you?"

She would have pulled her hand free, but he would not let her. And after a moment she stopped trying. She looked up at him and unshed tears seemed to well in her eyes.

"Oh, Julian! You mean well, I do not doubt that! But what you suggest, it would condemn us both to a lifetime of misery. You would forever be regretting the woman you truly cared for and I, I would be regretting that I had not had the resolution of character to refuse you."

"No!"

But she shook her head, even as she smiled a watery smile. "Oh, yes you would. You are asking me out of a sense of duty, nothing more. Yes, and because of our friendship. But you no more wish to marry me than you would my aunt. If you will not be sensible, then I must."

Julian took a deep breath. "I am not asking you out of duty!" he told her, and to his astonishment, he realized it was true. His voice held more conviction as he went on, "No, nor would I spend my life regretting the loss of Miss Winley, for that is who I collect you think I would miss. Pamela, I am asking you because this is what I want."

Still she shook her head and he wanted to shake her. But somehow he did not think that would advance his cause. And so he settled for taking a step backwards. His voice dripped icy dignity as he bowed and said, "I had no notion you had such a poor opinion of me, Miss Fairchild. I thought you knew me well enough to respect me as I respect you. My profound apologies. I shall not inflict my company on you any longer!"

And then he turned and left. He waited for her to call him back but her voice did not come and it was with profoundly lowered spirits that he rode home.

Behind him Pamela clenched her fists at her side. Had she made a horrible mistake? But how could she have acted other than as she did?

Pamela did not realize she had spoken aloud until Daphne spoke from one of the doorways that led off the main hall. "You could have accepted him at his word. I should have, in your place."

Stung, Pamela turned to her cousin and said, "You? You refused every suitor who offered for you!"

Daphne stiffened. "It was not the same. And perhaps it is precisely because of my mistakes that I do not wish to see you make the same."

And then she turned and was gone, leaving Pamela feeling lonelier than ever.

Was she destined, Lady Gwendolyn asked herself, to be forever overhearing conversations today? She waited until Pamela had gone into one of the parlors before she followed her daughter. She found Daphne in the billiard room. Richard was there as well and it was evident he had been drinking.

She paused in the doorway and looked at them, the children she loved so much, and thought how unnatural it was, the lives they led. To be sure, her brother, Lord Kendall, made Richard enough of an allowance that he could make short visits to London. No doubt he still hoped that sooner or later he would marry an heiress. But he had not done so and Lady Gwendolyn somehow doubted he ever would.

As for Daphne, she did not wish to go to London. That she made abundantly clear whenever asked. With a sigh, Lady Gwendolyn straightened her shoulders and stepped forward. She would know about the night of the ball. She would discover if Harry had returned.

What she would not be told, Lady Gwendolyn knew, what she might never know, was why, if he had, it would so haunt her children. They had not been willing to tell her when Harry was alive, nor anytime since, and she had no reason to think they would do so now.

Chapter 17

It ought to have been raining, Lady Kendall thought as she stared out the window the morning of the funeral. She would keep to her room today, she thought. Let whoever wished make of it what they would. What point was there to going downstairs? The men would attend the funeral and the women would gather to pretend that nothing important was happening.

Perhaps that was unfair. Perhaps they would gather and speculate upon the dead man's identity. And how he came to be dead in the library. Either way, Lady Kendall wanted none of it. So she stayed by the window, merely telling her maid to bring up a breakfast tray, though she doubted she would be able to eat. Still, it was important to keep up appearances. That was what her mother had always said.

Downstairs it was a somber grouping. The men, all dressed in black, ate quietly and talked in murmurs about the funeral ahead. Even Julian Deerwood made an appearance. He was pale, but determined to lend his support to the family. No one had the heart to turn him away. He saw Pamela in the hallway and gave her hand a quick squeeze of sympathy but there was no time to talk for the carriages were already waiting. The women watched them go and then retreated to the drawing room, a somber group themselves.

"I still cannot see why that unknown creature must be buried in the family plot!" Lady Gwendolyn declared tremulously, determined to keep to that pretense until the end. "It is an insult to all of us."

Lady Fairchild tried to soothe her. "Even you must see that the resemblance was too strong to deny. Surely you can see that it was wise to have the poor man buried as soon as possible, and had Lord Kendall not arranged it, he would still be lying, waiting for someone to do so."

But Lady Gwendolyn was not soothed. She turned angry eyes on Lady Fairchild. In her most austere voice she said, "You are not family, save by marriage. How can you pretend to know how we ought to feel?"

And then Lady Gwendolyn rose to her feet and strode from the room. Her daughter, Daphne, watched, catching her lower lip between her teeth. She seemed torn between wanting to apologize for her mother and following her. She settled for doing neither.

Lady Winley spoke from her corner of the room. "In general, I am not in favor of granting recognition to illegitimate children. In this case, however, I do believe that Lord Kendall showed proper feeling in arranging the burial as he did. You will no doubt wish to put it about that perhaps the creature was a heretofore unknown cousin or something of the sort."

No one bothered to answer her. Pamela and Catherine had their heads bent over fashion plates and Mrs. Merriweather knew well enough to hold her own counsel. Under other circumstances she might have agreed with Lady Winley. As it was, however, she could only trust that the truth would not destroy Anna or those she loved.

With a sigh, the former governess looked toward the window. How she wished that it were customary for women to attend funerals. There was much she might have learned by watching faces at the graveside. Even Andrew, had he been here, could have done so on her behalf. Instead she could only wait and wonder and worry about how she would best be able to help

Lady Fairchild. To that end, she moved to sit beside her former charge and they talked in quiet, soothing tones for some time.

Someone else had the same thought as Mrs. Merriweather. Sir Geoffrey certainly stared with great care at the faces of the family. And that of Julian Deerwood. He saw irritation, anger, fear, but no grief. Not for the dead man, at any rate, though Sir Geoffrey would have been willing to wager that a number of these men were feeling very sorry for themselves. It was a point of view he could not share.

These were gentlemen. He had dined with them in the past and perhaps would do so again. He had called Lord Fairchild his friend. It was the worst luck in the world that he had been called upon to deal with this murder. But he had been. And Sir Geoffrey found that he had a dislike of death, particularly violent death. And of any man who could take a life callously, as someone had done here. Because whatever else he might read on the faces before him, the one emotion that was notably absent was remorse.

After the body was buried, the crowd dispersed. And crowd it was for there was a great curiosity about the murder that had occurred up at the manor. But the family lingered. Sir Geoffrey shifted to stand behind them, in hopes they would think he had left and therefore talk more freely. To be sure, he could no longer see their faces but then neither could they see his. It seemed a fair trade to him. The family did not see it quite the same way.

It was Richard Avery who first realized he was still there and who took umbrage at his presence. "What the devil are you still hanging about for?" he demanded of Sir Geoffrey. "Hoping one of us will say something useful to you? Confess, perhaps?"

It did not ruffle the magistrate's mood. He shrugged.

"It would make matters easier all around if someone did," Sir Geoffrey said.

"And if we do not wish to make matters easier for you?" Avery persisted.

Sir Geoffrey looked him up and down and then said mildly, "I do not think, sir, that you could do so in any event."

Julian Deerwood reached out to prevent Avery from surging forward. "Enough," he said softly. "You must know he wishes you and your family to lose your tempers and betray yourselves."

"Quite right," Lord Kendall said, to Deerwood's mortification. "I suppose you didn't mean anyone to overhear but you are quite right. Richard, behave yourself. We shall not give Sir Geoffrey the satisfaction of seeing us lose control."

"You are very protective of your family," Sir Geoffrey observed.

"I am," Lord Kendall agreed. "All of my family. Including the man we buried today. I will not allow anyone to harm any of my family. I will do whatever is required to protect them."

The earl turned and looked at Deerwood then. "You may let my nephew go. And you may go home yourself. This desire to attach yourself to my family is very touching but I assure you that I am capable of protecting them all on my own. Including my granddaughter, Pamela. Do I make myself clear?"

But the younger man would not yield. "Perhaps you mean to do so, sir," he replied. "But the fact remains that two men are dead, dead on Kendall land. I will continue to give Pamela what support and protection I can."

The words were like a blow to Lord Kendall. He went pale and Lord Fairchild moved to support him. But the earl waved his son away. To Deerwood he said, "There have been failures, I will grant you. And I regret them deeply. But no matter how much I have failed any member of my family in the past, I will not fail my granddaughter. I will do whatever is necessary to keep her safe."

"Look at the sky," Lord Fairchild said, patently trying to distract everyone. "Let us go back to the house. A chill wind is blowing up and it looks as though it might rain. We had best be indoors if it does."

The men dispersed to the carriages and Sir Geoffrey watched them go. He eyed Richard Avery the longest. There was a young man with a temper, if ever he had seen one. He wondered how far he would go if pushed to the breaking point by a relative he did not like. Perhaps even one who could cut into what little inheritance there might be for him. He wished the information from the solicitor would arrive.

Then, of course, there was Lord Fairchild. For all the family's talk of by-blows, Sir Geoffrey believed the dead man was his lordship's twin, no matter how many swore they had seen him killed so many years ago. His lordship would have stood to lose a great deal if his brother suddenly reappeared. He seemed a good man, but many an apparently good man had been tempted to evil deeds to far less purpose than this would have been.

And Lord Kendall. What would he have thought if a beloved son were about to be replaced by one who had not been loved? One who had brought only scandal and disgrace to his name during the short time he had been alive? Or suppose this truly was a son born the wrong side of the blanket. What would the earl have done if such a one tried to come and demand money from him? Sir Geoffrey did not think the old man would have been likely to oblige. At least not willingly.

Then there were the women. To be sure, one would not think it likely that a lady would stab a gentleman with a letter opener. One might even wonder whether she would have the strength. But the earl did seem

very concerned about protecting his granddaughter.
Was it because he knew something about her? And
there was the other one. The Avery girl. She had, if
rumors were true, reason to want her cousin dead. If
it were he in the grave. And would Lady Gwendolyn
kill to avenge her daughter or because her nephew
had led her husband to ruin?

Or could it have been Lady Fairchild? Would she
kill to protect her husband's title and wealth? Or suppose it was not Fairchild's twin but, as the family said
they believed, a by-blow of the earl? Could Lady Kendall have killed one of her husband's illegitimate offspring in a fit of rage?

And what about Lady Winley and her daughter? It
seemed most unlikely they could be involved in this.
And yet, their appearance here seemed a bit odd, ac-
cording to the servants. And there seemed to be no
love lost between them and the family. So could Lady
Winley or her daughter have some reason to wish the
man dead? Or perhaps to wish Lord Fairchild dead,
since the resemblance was so great?

The only person Sir Geoffrey was willing to concede
could not be the murderer was Mrs. Merriweather,
and that was from what he knew of her when she had
been a governess plus the manner in which she had
conducted herself the day of the death and since. Still,
if someone were to bring him evidence to the contrary,
Sir Geoffrey would reconsider at once.

No, he thought with a sigh, he was no closer to
being sure about the murderer than before. He
thought it must be Lord Fairchild, but when he saw
them all together, he wondered. And Sir Geoffrey was
not a man to like uncertainty.

Well, there were things being done, and soon he
might have some answers. Thank heavens no one had
noticed that Fairchild's brother's grave had been disturbed. The last thing Sir Geoffrey wanted was for
them to be forewarned; the last thing he needed was

for them to be even angrier with him than they already were.

Slowly Sir Geoffrey made his way to his own carriage and directed his coachman to drive up to Kendall Hall. They wouldn't be happy to see him, but he needed to speak with Mrs. Merriweather. With luck, he would manage to do so in private and the family need never know he had been there. Except, of course, that the servants would almost certainly tell them. But that could not be helped.

Richard Avery found Catherine waiting for him when he went to the outbuilding where he kept his private supply of brandy, taken from the Earl of Kendall's stock. Immediately he glanced toward the house, only too aware that they could be seen from there if anyone bothered to look. But she didn't seem to care.

"I need your answer," she said. "You must marry me! And soon!"

For once, Richard was too tired to pretend. Too tired to think of pretty words to tease her into a better mood. He merely looked at her and said, "No."

Catherine stared back. "You cannot mean it!" she whispered.

He scuffed his foot in the dirt. His head ached abominably for he, like the other men in the household, had been indulging freely in the brandy the moment they returned from the funeral and now he wanted more. More than his family would let him have.

"You must see it won't work," he told her. "Your father said he would cut you off without a penny if we married. And if he did that, my grandfather would cease to give me the allowance he gives me now. They've both made that plain enough!"

"But if they knew?"

"If they knew, they would still cast us both off without a penny and then where would we be?"

"But isn't it worth a push?" she demanded. "What am I to do?"

"I don't know!"

She stared at him then half turned away. Over her shoulder she said, "Perhaps I should marry Deerwood."

"You don't mean that!"

"Why not? He would take me quick enough and I can tell him whatever tale I like afterwards. He won't turn against me, no matter what he suspects."

Richard Avery stared at her for a long moment, but he didn't speak. Finally she turned on her heel and walked away. And as she went, Catherine felt a sense of despair. It wasn't easy to grow up at seventeen and face the fact that one wasn't a heedless child anymore, but she would do it.

Neither she nor Richard saw the woman watching from the house. They would not have cared, had they done so. What, after all, was a former governess to them?

Mrs. Merriweather was tempted to go down and speak with Miss Winley, for she had a strong notion she knew what the animated discussion seen from her window must mean. Obviously the two young people needed her help. Indeed, she had excused herself to Lady Fairchild and was halfway down the stairs when Sir Geoffrey was shown in.

He saw her on the stairs and said in a genial tone, "Mrs. Merriweather? Might I have a word with you? In private?"

"Of course, sir." She turned to the major domo. "I believe we may use this room here?"

Damford nodded, if not approvingly, at least signifying consent. Mrs. Merriweather was careful, however, to make certain she closed the door completely and then move with Sir Geoffrey to the far side of

the room, to deter eavesdroppers, before they began
to speak.

"Did anyone notice the late Lord Fairchild's grave
had been disturbed?" Mrs. Merriweather asked.

Sir Geoffrey shook his head. "No, we were fortunate that they were distracted by other matters and
did not wish, with me there to see, to show too great
an interest in his graveside." He paused, then added,
"There was a body in the coffin."

"His?"

The magistrate shrugged. "After so long, who can
be certain?"

For a moment they were silent. When they spoke,
it was at the same moment, with the same words.

"Did anyone say anything useful?"

They smiled at each other and Sir Geoffry indicated that Mrs. Merriweather should go first. "Lady
Kendall did not appear. Lady Gwendolyn took exception to the burial in the family plot. Mrs. Winley was
surprisingly polite. Lady Fairchild seemed bewildered
by it all. And the young ladies all tried to pretend a
funeral was not taking place."

Sir Geoffrey nodded. Then he gave his own sum-
mary and concluded, "Not one of the men was sorry
to see the fellow buried, whoever he might be. They
said what one might expect. Indeed, the most interesting exchange was when young Deerwood was told to
take himself off, that he wasn't needed. He said he
was there to show support for Miss Fairchild. The old
earl took exception to what he perceived as a slight
concerning his ability to look after his own."

"He is a touchy fellow," Mrs. Merriweather agreed.
"Well, I cannot say I am surprised, but I do not see
how any of it brings you closer to a solution. I find
myself wishing that something certain would reveal
itself. I greatly dislike having to suspect every person
around me of being capable of murder."

Sir Geoffrey gave her a brief smile. "I might very

well say the same but I cannot think it likely to happen simply because we wish it would."

"No," she agreed reluctantly. "We shall have to make a push to find the answer ourselves."

That gave the magistrate pause. He looked at her closely. "You are cautious since the night you were attacked?" Sir Geoffrey said with some concern.

Mrs. Merriweather smiled, but it was not a pleasant smile. "Oh, yes," she said. "Most cautious. I've no wish to make a third victim."

"Good. Well, I'd best be going. Send word if you discover anything new."

"I shall."

He started to go, then paused and looked at her one more time, his gaze a searching one. "Mrs. Merriweather," he said gently, "do not think you can protect Lady Fairchild, if you discover that either she or someone dear to her committed these murders. I shall discover the truth, you know."

She drew herself up to her full, diminutive height. Her voice was austere as she replied, "My dear Sir Geoffrey, I believe I know my duty."

"I hope you do," he said and then he was gone, leaving a very troubled Mrs. Merriweather behind.

Pamela hesitated. She knew her grandmother might not wish to be disturbed, but it was very unlike her not to come downstairs at all today. And while she had never felt as close a connection to Lady Kendall as she did to her grandfather, nonetheless she was worried about her. So it was that she found herself gently knocking at her grandmother's door to check on her.

"Come in."

Pamela was reassured to hear the strength in Lady Kendall's voice. The sight that greeted her, however, did not match the voice. Her grandmother sat by the window, dressed in deepest black bombazine, and in her lap she held a book she instantly closed at the sight of Pamela. Her color was pale and her lips trembled, but the eyes were defiant as she greeted her granddaughter.

"Well? What is it? A crisis that needs my attention? Some trouble with the servants that needs to be sorted out? Speak up, child, tell me what the problem is!"

Pamela slowly closed the door behind her and advanced into the room until she stood right in front of her grandmother. She had meant to ask her if the dead man was her uncle, Harry. But she could not, not now. Instead she knelt down and put her hands over Lady Kendall's trembling ones.

"I came to see if you were all right, Grandmama. It is so unlike you, you see, to keep to your rooms like this. I wanted to see if there was anything I could do for you."

Lady Kendall tried to shrug off the concern. "I am merely tired, that is all."

Despite herself, Pamela laughed. "You have never been tired in your life!"

"Well, I am now," Lady Kendall retorted crossly even as she pulled her hands free.

"It's the dead man, isn't it?" Pamela said gently. "You know who he is and you grieve for him. But you don't wish us asking questions, so you do it up here where no one will see. Who was he?"

It was as close as she could come to asking. And for a long moment she feared she had pushed her grandmother too far. Lady Kendall's face was very gray and she did not speak. Pamela began to believe the older woman wasn't going to answer her. But finally she did, the words coming slowly.

"It doesn't matter who he was. Not really. You could see by his face he must be family, of one sort or another."

"Who killed him? Do you know?"

Pamela didn't know where the words had come

from but now Lady Kendall looked at her, her eyes bleaker than ever. Her voice was scarcely louder than a whisper as she replied, "I don't know. I don't want to know. I only know it must have been someone who believed he—or perhaps she—was protecting us, protecting the family."

Pamela wanted to question her more, to ask how anyone could think death would protect the family. She might, given a little more time, even have gotten up the courage to ask if her grandmother thought the dead man had been Uncle Harry.

But Lady Kendall abruptly stood. "Go away now, Pamela," she said. Her voice was cold and forbidding. "I wish to be alone."

There was nothing for her granddaughter to do but obey.

Chapter 18

The next morning began when the household was roused early by the screams of one of the servants. When Pamela first heard the sound, she considered hiding in her room and not going to find out what was wrong. But she had never been a coward and she would not begin now. So she hastily dressed and went to see.

Fortunately, it was a housemaid starting at shadows in the gallery who screamed. She had mistaken the drape of a curtain over a chair for a body. Nothing to cause the least alarm. But it was a measure of how shaken the entire household felt that such a mistake was made in the first place.

Every face was pale, almost every person trembling at least a little. Except Mrs. Merriweather. She stood beside Pamela's mother, speaking quietly to Lady Fairchild. And Pamela's grandfather, the earl, was as calm as usual. But then nothing had ever been known to discompose the man. It was a matter of often-stated pride to him that it should be so. And while she understood, it was to her mother and her mother's former governess that Pamela instinctively moved closer.

Mrs. Merriweather was dressed with her usual care, not the scrambled manner in which almost everyone else had appeared. Now she smiled reassuringly at Pamela and said, "You may as well go back to your room and tidy up, my dear. There is nothing more to be seen here. It looks to have been a prank, nothing more."

"Do you think so?" Lady Fairchild asked hopefully.

Someone else overheard them. "A prank?" Lord Fairchild echoed indignantly. "Who the devil would do such a thing? And why should you think it anything more than a silly maid's mistake?"

Mrs. Merriweather shrugged. "I think it because a drape would not be likely to fall, of its own accord, over the chair just so. No, I should judge it to have been carefully arranged. As to why, one must suppose the person thought it would be amusing to frighten whoever mistook it, as it was meant to be mistaken, for a body. I shall not even try to guess who it might have been, for I do not know this household well enough to try."

"A footman," Lady Fairchild suggested. "Perhaps one of the footmen thought it would be amusing to frighten the housemaids?"

"Perhaps."

One word that conveyed all her derisive doubt. But Mrs. Merriweather refused to say more. Instead she moved away from the crowd saying, in a far more prosaic tone, "I wonder if breakfast has yet been laid out downstairs? Will anyone join me?"

With mutterings about insensitive old women, the others turned their backs on her. All except Lady Fairchild, who kept close to her side. Pamela looked from the rest of her family to Mrs. Merriweather and back again. Finally she fled to her room to tidy up as quickly as she could and then she all but ran down to the breakfast parlor in hopes of finding the former governess alone.

Unfortunately, Pamela was not the only one to have had the notion of joining Mrs. Merriweather. Whether it was because they wished to keep an eye on her and overhear anything else she might say, or because they were hungry, most of the family was in the breakfast parlor, shooting daggers with their eyes at her. How far their rudeness might have gone could not be said, for Lady Winley and her daughter were also present. They had not come to the gallery when the maid screamed, but it was evident that was what had roused them. And none of the family cared to air their grievances with Mrs. Merriweather before these two women.

It was not a very comfortable meal, but it was a hearty one for no one wished to be the first to leave the room and risk missing anything. Thus it was Mrs. Merriweather who was the first to rise from the table. As she did so, she said absentmindedly, as though to herself, "I think I shall spend the morning in writing letters."

The moment she was gone, the family proceeded to rip her character to shreds.

"Impertinent creature!"

"Much too far above herself!"

"A former governess! Really, Anna, I cannot conceive why you thought it necessary or right to invite her here."

But Mama refused to be routed, Pamela thought with pride. She continued to eat and refused to respond to anyone. Eventually the others tired of the game and left the breakfast parlor in disgust. At last it was only the two of them, Pamela and Lady Fairchild.

Now Mama looked at her and said quietly, "I hope you will not listen to them. It is only fear speaking. Miss Tibbles, that is to say Mrs. Merriweather, has always been a woman of sense, and right now, we need sense in this household. I fear for what may happen otherwise."

"I like her," was all Pamela said.

Mama nodded. "Good. I know you are having difficulties of your own, for I have seen how you look at Deerwood and how he has looked at Miss Winley. You may find Mrs. Merriweather to possess a useful ear. Despite her demeanor, she can be surprisingly kind upon occasion. Indeed, I think I shall go and seek her out myself. I could use a little of her kindness this morning."

Then, before Pamela could tell her that she already had spoken with Mrs. Merriweather, Mama rose and walked from the room. It hurt to see the way she seemed to have aged in the past two months and Pamela wondered what troubled her. But she knew better than to ask. Neither Mama nor Papa thought her old enough to confide in nor, Pamela suspected, did they confide in each other these days. Which worried her most of all for, until now, the two had been scandalously close. They had been solicitous of one another and shared everything. Or so it seemed to the child she had been.

Had she been so mistaken in what she thought she saw then or was she mistaken now? Had some calamity occurred to cause such a breach between them?

Whatever the answer, Pamela felt as though her world had been shaken. As though she no longer knew what was true and what was not. She no longer felt the certainty that life was benevolent and fate had smiled upon her as once she did. No, now she began to wonder if the Fairchilds were cursed. For surely nothing could be more appalling than the events of the past week.

It was in just such a mood that Pamela encountered Julian Deerwood. He was shown into the breakfast parlor as she was sipping the last of her morning tea. At her look of surprise, Damford said, "I did not think you would mind, Miss Fairchild, Mr. Deerwood as having been so much like family all these years."

"Yes, of course, Damford," Pamela replied.

And yet she did not think of Julian as family. No, she coveted something much more from him, and it was the knowledge that he could, he must, regard her only as a sister, however many times he might offer for her, that gave her the greatest pain.

But today he did not apparently mean to renew his suit, as she had feared he would. Instead, he strode to the table and sank into the chair beside hers. When a servant appeared with a clean plate for Julian, he waved the fellow away.

"Leave us," he said. "I wish to speak to Miss Fairchild in private."

The servant did as he was asked, for Lady Pamela was a favorite in this household and all the servants wished her well. Even in the midst of the family troubles, they thought it only right that she should have her shot at happiness. And from the fervency in his tone, Mr. Deerwood must have finally come to realize his own heart in the matter.

If he knew what the fellow thought, Julian gave no sign of it. Indeed, he seemed scarcely to notice anything save his own harried thoughts. And now he spoke them aloud to her.

"They are saying in the village that Sir Geoffrey is about to arrest your father for murder," he said in gentle, measured tones.

Without quite knowing how, Pamela found herself on her feet. "No. This cannot be."

But she knew only too well that it could. Not that she believed her father capable of such violence but arrested, yes, that was all too possible.

Julian came to grasp her shoulders. "Don't worry. It will all come to nothing. It must. But I wished you to have some warning. Whatever happens, you know that I shall stand by you."

Even in the midst of her own pain, Pamela looked up at him and smiled. She touched the side of his cheek with her hand. "You are such a dear, sweet friend, Julian. But I cannot ask such a thing of you. Go. See Miss Winley. Follow her to London, if need be, to patch up your quarrel. I'll not have you unhappy because of me."

He did not argue. Not as he had the day before.

And Pamela felt a tiny twist in her heart at his silence. Then he spoke. His voice was gentle and almost chiding.

"If our places were reversed, would you desert me? Would you follow a man to London and leave me bereft?"

Pamela could not meet his eyes or answer him, but Julian went on anyway. "Of course you would not! I wonder that you think so much less of me."

"But I don't!" she cried.

That was all the encouragement he needed. He lifted both her hands to his lips and kissed them. "I am glad to hear you say so. For I should be very hurt if you did not. As for Miss Winley, I have come to understand that I was mistaken. Both in her and in myself. I have no regrets in watching her go, I assure you."

Pamela desperately wanted to believe him. And for just this short space of time, she thought, perhaps it would be all right not to argue with him? To let him stand by her? To take the comfort he offered? She leaned toward him, her face tilted up to his. And it was at that inopportune moment Damford intruded.

"Er, Lady Pamela, my apologies but the earl is asking for you."

"I must go," she said to Julian.

He squeezed her hands once more then released them. "Of course."

She moved past him and toward the stairs. Behind her Damford coughed, and when she turned to look at him, he explained, "He is in the library."

Pamela nodded and changed direction, a little of her anxiety eased by this. For if he felt well enough to come downstairs, she need not worry quite so much about his health. And indeed when she went into the library, she found that if he was not smiling, nevertheless her grandfather was more at ease than she had seen him since before the masquerade ball.

Still, there was a degree of concern in her voice as she asked, "How are you today?"

He shrugged. "As well as may be with the household at sixes and sevens! Ah, well, it will all blow over."

"Will it?" she asked doubtfully.

"It had better!" the earl said firmly as he waved her to a seat near him.

The chessboard was already set up and he quirked an eyebrow at her. "Ready for a game?"

"With you?" she teased. "Never! You will sadly trounce me and we both know it."

"Do we?" he retorted, the gentleness creeping into his voice despite his best attempts to keep it out. "And here I have been telling myself that you always let me win out of affection for my person and respect for my age."

Pamela could not help herself nor did she try. She reached out and placed her hand over his. "I wish," she said with all the openness in her heart, "that I might be so clever. But you have never needed my help for anything."

He caught her hand with his. "There you are out! I need your company. It is sunshine to me. And I do not know what I shall do, what any of us shall do, when once you are wed and gone from Kendall Hall."

Pamela reached out to move a pawn, for it was always their habit that she should go first. "That is not likely to be for some time," she said firmly.

"No? I am told young Deerwood might have other notions."

With a lightness she wished she could truly feel, Pamela laughed. "If he had his way, it would be so. At least today. By next week he may have fixed his interest on some other young lady."

"And you would not mind?"

Pamela hesitated. "I know you would not like the match, that it is not grand enough for you."

But the earl shook his head. "You mistake me for your grandmother. She is the one with all the ambition for her grandchildren. It is true I have reservations about the match but only because I wish to see all of my grandchildren happy. Especially you, my dear."

What was there to say to that? Pamela would have looked away in confusion, but the habit of respect was too strong for her to do other than meet his eyes as squarely as his met hers. And to smile a wry, crooked smile.

"Well then, we are well paired, sir, for I should dearly like to see you happy."

His expression turned dark then. And he sighed. He looked older than even moments before. "That, my dear, is not likely to happen so long as these deaths hang over our heads."

Pamela leaned toward him. "What do you think happened, Grandfather? You are the shrewdest man I know, surely you have some guess?"

He hesitated, then sighed again. "I wish I could tell you, my dear. But I confess I have not bent my mind to the task of discovering the truth. Perhaps it is old age, or perhaps fear of what I should learn. In any event, I am declaring it a privilege of age and rank to leave all investigation to Sir Geoffrey."

Pamela understood. She understood too well. But she could not leave it at that point.

"I fear the answer also, Grandfather. But is it not preferable to know? At least then we should only have to fear one person, grieve for one person turned wrong. As it stands, we must all look at everyone and wonder."

The earl snorted. "Wonder what?"

But she would not be silenced, not even by her beloved grandfather. "We must wonder who and why and whether any of us are in danger from that person. We must wonder what further secrets will be revealed and who will be hurt to prevent it. We must wonder how terrible the final answers will be."

"With luck, we need never know any of it, and in time, it will blow over and we can go on with our lives as before," he said gruffly.

"You don't really mean that, sir. Not really. You are just afraid. But have you not always taught me that I must look life straight in the face? And face facts no matter how painful?"

He grimaced. "So I have," he conceded. "And now you are throwing my own words up to me. Well, it is no more than I should have expected. Very well, since you will have it so, I shall bend my mind to the task of trying to figure out who did these murders."

"And why," Pamela persisted.

"And why."

With a sense that a weight had been lifted off her shoulders, Pamela turned her attention back to the chessboard, and for at least a little while, she and her grandfather were able to forget the problems of the present in contemplation of the game.

Chapter 19

Julian Deerwood was standing in the gardens, trying to decide whether he ought to wait for Pamela or simply go back home, when an elegantly clad young lady rounded the hedge. She had taken more care than usual with her appearance, he thought, and he could not help but wonder who it was for.

Even as he wondered, Miss Catherine Winley came toward him and held out her hand. "Julian! There you are! They said you were here but I could not find you anywhere within the house. Why did you not simply ask for me?"

Julian gaped at her. Why the devil was she being so nice to him? He could not ask her, of course, but neither could he entirely trust this new kindness of hers. It was so unlike how she had treated him of late. But then, he thought grimly, perhaps she thought him her best chance of entertainment. After all, it had not been that long since she complained about the lack of parties and such at the hall.

But he said none of this aloud. There was a part of him that did not care what her motive might be. A part of his heart that simply was too glad that she was smiling at him, pretending to be glad to see him.

He held out a hand and she took it and allowed him to lead her to the bench. She settled herself and then smiled coyly at him as she repeated, "Why did you not ask for me?"

"I, er, I thought you would not agree to see me,"

he said, scrambling to find coherent words with which to answer her. "After all, we did not part on the best of terms the last time we spoke."

She waved away the objection as though it were nothing. Which perhaps, to her, it was. She managed a trilling laugh. "Oh surely you did not take seriously what I said? Besides, I am allowed to change my mind, am I not?"

"Yes, of course."

"Good. I knew you would think so. Tell me, when do you return to London?" Then, before he could answer, she added archly, "Mama means to return as soon as may be. Though that rude magistrate says we must wait."

With some constraint, Julian replied, "I cannot, I will not leave so long as Miss Fairchild's family is in such distress."

Her eyes seemed to narrow in displeasure but he told himself he must be mistaken in thinking so. He could not, however, pretend he misunderstood her next words.

"And do I play no part in your decision?" she asked in the arch voice he had once thought so endearing.

But now Julian stared at her as though he had never seen Miss Winley before. And perhaps he had not. Very carefully he said, "Miss Fairchild's troubles must be of primary concern to all her friends. I could not desert her until they are resolved and that is, that must be, the basis for any decision I make."

"But why?" Catherine asked, her eyes wide. "It is not as though they are your troubles! Although I have heard you met one of the dead men." She shivered and leaned toward him. "That must have been such a strange feeling."

"I did not know, when I met him, that he would be killed within the day," Julian pointed out dryly. "I only thought him a strange fellow."

Catherine touched his arm. "Yes, but it must have seemed strange, when you heard about his death."

Before Julian could answer, Mrs. Merriweather appeared, a determined look upon her face.

"Miss Winley? I should like to speak with you, please."

Catherine blinked at Mrs. Merriweather but was too surprised to do anything other than rise to her feet and follow the other woman. She did, however, turn and smile at Julian as she left.

Somewhat to her surprise, Mrs. Merriweather did not lead the way to the house but rather toward the folly. Once there she seated herself, indicated that Catherine should do so as well, and then said briskly, "What did you think you were trying to do with Mr. Deerwood? I thought you wished to marry Mr. Avery."

Catherine looked down at her hands. She hesitated.

"I truly do wish to help," Mrs. Merriweather said gently.

"I know it," Catherine agreed. "And I do wish to marry Mr. Avery. It is just . . ."

"Go on, my dear."

"He does not believe we can! And I am desperate!" Catherine blurted out.

"Why? You need not scruple to tell me. I can hold my tongue and have done so many times. Why are you desperate, my dear?"

Again, Catherine hesitated. Her eyes were full of tears. "I can't tell you," she whispered. But in the end, she did.

The former governess listened quietly, nodded several times, then rose to her feet and said, "I thought such might be the case. But Mr. Deerwood is not the answer, I assure you. I shall go and speak to Mr. Avery. There is a solution and I hope I may help him to find it."

It was absurd to believe this little woman could do

so much, but Catherine did so anyway. As she rose to her feet to accompany Mrs. Merriweather back to the house, she felt her spirits to be unaccountably lighter.

Pamela had felt her heart contract as she watched Julian and Miss Winley seated side by side on the bench. For all his protestations earlier, he seemed content enough to be with her now. Except that perhaps he was not. He did not seem to smile at her in precisely the same way he had when she first arrived. Nor did he gaze at her with the look in his eyes that had caused Pamela so much pain.

Indeed, the more she thought about it, the closer she regarded the pair, the more it looked as if Julian felt some discomfort, seated so close to Miss Winley. He seemed almost to be frowning at her.

To be sure, Pamela could not hear what they were saying, she was too far away for that, but Julian did not look like a young man besotted by the woman he was with. And a tiny flame of hope lit inside a secret corner of her heart. Perhaps, after all, it was possible he had meant what he said, that he had come to feel for her what she felt for him.

Still, it was hard not to curl her hands into fists at the sight of Miss Winley touching his arm and smiling up at him so charmingly. And the more Pamela thought about it, the odder that seemed. For she would swear the smile did not reach the other girl's eyes.

Then Mrs. Merriweather appeared and Pamela caught just a hint of panic in Miss Winley's expression before the girl carefully made her expression blank. What on earth was going on here?

Pamela meant to slip away before she was seen. She did not wish, after all, for Julian to think she was spying upon him. But before she could do so, something made him look her way. And then there was nothing to be done except to go forward and greet him.

He rose to meet her but paused to glance over his shoulder in the direction Miss Winley had gone and blush. Pamela wanted to smile at him. Foolish man! Did he think she would care who he talked to, so long as his heart was hers? Did he understand so little about her?

Perhaps. So it was more kindly than she had intended that she greeted him now. And answered his stammered question about the earl's health.

"Oh, Grandfather is in excellent spirits today. Indeed, I think he will outlive us all, and so I tell him! He simply wished to play chess."

"Did he win?" Julian asked with a smile, knowing how intense their games could be.

"Oh, yes. Of course he did. Though he has begun to suspect that I make sure he does. I fobbed him off this time, but it cannot last. I suppose I shall have to begin to win a few times, just to throw him off the scent."

Julian laughed. "You are very kind to him."

"How could I not be?" Pamela asked, tucking her hand into his elbow as they began to walk toward the roses. "My grandfather has been all kindness to me since I was a tiny child, patiently enduring my company when the other adults would have sent me back to the nursery. He has never tried to curb my temperament or told me that I must be this or that simply because I am a girl and a lady. He has always encouraged me to follow every interest and been willing to debate with me all those things Mama and Papa would tell me were beyond the understanding of a female. Who else has entered into my sentiments in such a way?"

Julian smiled down at her. "I have."

Pamela pinched his arm. "Yes, but you are not family so you do not count."

"Not count?" Julian pretended to be offended. "But I am an unmarried gentleman! Did your mother not tell you I am to be placated at all costs?"

"I should not listen if she did," Pamela told him honestly. "I value your opinion, of course, but you cannot understand what it has meant to have an ally within my home with the power to silence my parents when they would have made me into someone I am not."

Abruptly Julian sobered. "I think perhaps I do. For you remember how my parents pushed me to court the daughter of our neighbor on the other side of Father's estate. Had she not married someone else, they would still be doing so."

For the briefest moment Pamela rested her head against his shoulder. "We have both been sorely put upon by our families. And we have both encouraged each other. There can be no better recommendation of a friend."

"Or perhaps a man and wife?" Julian asked, pausing to look down at her.

Pamela caught her breath at the look in his eyes. A look she had long since despaired of ever seeing turned in her direction. A look she knew must be mirrored in her own. And when he dipped his head to capture her lips with his, she could make no protest, nor did she want to make one.

Later she could not have said whether it was his arms that pulled her close, or hers that wrapped around his neck first. She could not have said who deepened the kiss or who was the first to break free.

All she knew was that for both of them, their breaths came in shaky gasps and there was a new bond between them, a bond she had waited and hoped for all her life, it seemed.

"I think," he said, attempting to sound calm, "that I had best take you back to the house. It would not do for us to forget our circumstances."

"No, indeed!" Pamela agreed.

They did not even need to speak to know it was best that they not touch each other as they walked, side by side, to the hall. Nor that Julian ought to take his leave once he saw her safely to the door.

So bemused was she, that at first Pamela did not notice the commotion in the grand hall. There was a gentleman there. He had evidently just arrived and he was a stranger to her but not to Mrs. Merriweather. The former governess gave a tiny cry and moved forward to throw herself into the newcomer's arms. Mama stood watching, beaming with delight.

"Andrew! What are you doing here?"

The gentleman chuckled. "Marian, my love, did you truly think I would not come? One dead body might be ignored, perhaps, but two?"

Pamela watched with fascination as the brisk woman she had come to know turned into a gentle, almost pretty blushing woman as she looked up at the gentleman. Then, as though recollecting they were not alone, Mrs. Merriweather turned and looked about and drew the gentleman over to Pamela and her mother.

"This is Lady Fairchild. And her daughter, Miss Fairchild," she told the gentleman. To both Pamela and her mother she said, "Lady Fairchild, Miss Fairchild, this is my husband, Colonel Merriweather."

He bowed over Lady Fairchild's hand and greeted her. Then he turned to Pamela and grinned so beguilingly that she could easily understand Mrs. Merriweather's affection for this man.

"How do you do, my dear?" he asked kindly. "I know it must feel as though you are all under siege. Think of me as reinforcements, if you will."

"Thank you, sir," Pamela replied, feeling herself smile in return. "You are very kind."

He waved a hand. "Pish tosh. M'wife is the one who is kind. I merely tag along when she will allow it and lend her my support. Come, Marian, and show me where our daughter is. I have not seen her in far too long and am eager to know how she is doing."

Pamela watched them go up the stairs and found herself thinking that it would be very nice to feel about her future husband as they so clearly did about each other. Would it be that way for her, as it had been for her mother and father? If she and Julian did indeed marry, she thought perhaps it might be. At the very least, it was a pleasant thought to contemplate.

Chapter 20

As they approached the nursery, Mrs. Merriweather tried to warn the colonel.

"Nurse will not like it. She hates to have her routine disrupted and will refuse to let us see our daughter."

"Nonsense!" the colonel said briskly. "One simply has to know what to say."

Marian gave up the attempt and simply led the way. Once she had stepped inside the nursery, however, she let Andrew go ahead of her. Nurse, of course, bristled at the sight of intruders into her domain.

Immediately Andrew bowed. "Forgive me, madam! I know it is unconscionable of us to disrupt your routine, but I have come some distance and just arrived, and while I know I ought not to do so, I could not resist coming to see my daughter. And the wonderful woman who has been taking care of her."

To Marian's astonishment, the nurse blushed and curtsied. "It is no trouble, sir, I assure you. I shall fetch little Elizabeth at once. She is an angel and quite a favorite with me, you must know."

Andrew beamed at the woman, positively beamed. "Excellent! The good reports I have had of you are patently true."

And then the woman smiled at him. Marian thought her jaw must hit the floor, it was opened so wide in stunned surprise. Hastily she shut it. If Andrew could accomplish such a miracle with one servant, she thought, what might he do if she put him onto the

others in the household? What might he learn about
the murders?

But Andrew wasn't thinking about murders. He was
thinking about his daughter. And Marian felt foolishly
happy as she watched him laugh and play with their
child. He had no hesitation cooing at her, nor holding
her close. He did not care who might see his affection
for her and know that he was a doting father.

They left the nursery a short time later, with Nurse
saying they might visit at any time. Andrew was understandably pleased with himself, and if the truth be
told, Marian was rather pleased with him as well.

In her room, she greeted him more warmly than
would have been seemly in the main hall. Then she
said, "Why did you come?"

He quirked an eyebrow. "Did you think I would
not? The moment I read your letter I knew I had to
come and make certain you and Elizabeth were safe.
Now tell me everything."

She did so. And in telling him, clarified in her own
mind a number of details. When she was done, he
shook his head. "This is a bad business. A very bad
business. I remember a Fairchild in the military. But
not for long. He was booted out in a matter of days.
No one quite knows why, but he was an out-and-out
bounder. Question is, was it this Fairchild? Or could
it have been the other, the twin you told me about?"

"I think it more likely it was the other brother, the
one who was killed in a duel a year or two after Lady
Fairchild married her husband. I believe he was in the
military," Marian replied.

The colonel nodded. "I shall see what I can discover
at dinner if I find an excuse to talk about my experi-
ences. See if anyone finds the military fascinating or
mentions a Fairchild who purchased a commission."

"I shall depend upon it!" Marian told him. "Yes,
and I shall also depend upon you to turn up the servants sweet as well. They have unaccountably taken

me in dislike and I can discover nothing. But you handled that nurse as neatly as anything I have ever seen. And I am hoping that some of them not only know what has been going on in this house but will be willing to tell you about it. They don't talk to my maid, Kate, you see, not about these sorts of things, and someone must find out what they know. I do not scruple to tell you that I worry for Anna and Lord Fairchild."

He nodded. "I shall do everything I can to help."

If the family was surprised to have Colonel Merriweather arrive without invitation, they were too polite to say so. More, there was almost an air of relief that there was a new face in their company, someone entirely untouched by the grim deaths. Nor did they disdain to ask him about his part in the fight against Napoleon. Now that the tyrant was safely locked away, such stories took on a gallantry untouched by the fear they would have had just a few years before.

To be sure, Lady Winley meant to give him the cut, but that was before she discovered he was nephew to one of her bosom bows and that he still moved in the best circles, when he chose to do so. If Catherine hung on his words and listened with rapt admiration as he described the valor of the officers he had served with, well, perhaps it was all to the good if it gave her thoughts a different direction than young Deerwood.

And since it turned out that Lord Fairchild knew some of the men Colonel Merriweather had served with, a bond was soon formed between the two. Indeed, they seemed scarcely to notice as the ladies retired from the table after dinner. A point upon which Lady Kendall commented when they reached the drawing room.

"Really, I do not know what it is about men and war. It is as though they believe they are still playing with toy soldiers! And the number of silly young girls whose heads are turned by a uniform is absurd!"

She glared at Mrs. Merriweather as she said this. Lady Fairchild, who was sitting beside her former governess, was moved to protest on her friend's behalf. "But Miss Tibbles was scarcely a young girl when she met the colonel."

"No, and that makes it all the worse," Lady Gwendolyn said in acid tones. "She ought to have known better!"

Another woman might have become indignant, might have tried to defend herself. Mrs. Merriweather merely got an odd little smile upon her face and tilted her head to one side. "Do you know, I have never seen him in uniform? I wonder if I ought to ask him to don one just so I could see what he would look like if he did."

The others in the room gaped at her but Lady Winley's eyes narrowed and her voice was filled with condescension as she appeared to address everyone save Mrs. Merriweather, "Really, one cannot expect a person with so many years in service to have the same sensibilities as a true lady."

There was dead silence after that pronouncement. The ladies looked everywhere save at Mrs. Merriweather or Lady Winley. Instinctively they drew back from both. But no explosion appeared to occur. Instead Mrs. Merriweather began to laugh.

"Oh, I have heard about you, Lady Winley! So many times, over the years, I have heard about you. I would not have spoken for the world, for I do not believe in savaging another's character. But since you have no hesitation in attempting to savage mine, then I take leave to tell you that you are and always have been a fool, Minerva Winley! Full of self-importance and apparent propriety. When all the world knew otherwise."

"How dare you say such things?" Lady Winley demanded indignantly.

Mrs. Merriweather smiled seraphically. Her voice was gentle but amused as she replied, almost apologetically, "Well, you see, I have seen your third son."

Lady Winley went first very pale and then very red and then she rose to her feet. For a moment it seemed she would flee the room. Or demand that Mrs. Merriweather do so. But before she could make up her mind to do one or the other, the drawing room door opened and the men trooped in. And then it was too late. Lady Winley abruptly sat back down, and though she said not another word nor met anyone's eyes, she stayed. As did Mrs. Merriweather.

The gentlemen had consumed a sufficient quantity of spirits that they were in an almost jovial mood. Lady Kendall immediately called them to task for it.

"I see no reason for levity! Do you gentlemen think it amusing, perhaps, that two people are dead?"

Lord Kendall and Colonel Merriweather exchanged glances and Richard Avery merely flung himself into the chair farthest from his grandmother and sulked.

The colonel sat himself down beside his wife, murmured with her for a few minutes, then turned to Lady Fairchild. She regarded him with some surprise. He smiled.

"I have long been curious," he said, "to meet some of Mrs. Merriweather's pupils, and you, I understand, were her first. I should like to know what she was like in those days."

Lady Fairchild caught the spirit of his mood. Her eyes sparkled as she glanced at Mrs. Merriweather and said, in a teasing tone, "Oh, Miss Tibbles was absolutely terrifying! I dared not cross her for fear that I should find a bucket of cold water dumped over my head. Or something wriggly in my bed."

"Something wriggly?"

"Worms," Lady Fairchild replied succinctly. "Oh,

yes, Miss Tibbles had me terrified!" She leaned closer
and said, "I imagined all sorts of things about her. I
told myself she must have suffered a severe disap-
pointment in love."

The colonel made a sympathetic sound. "If she was
so terrifying," he said, "I wonder that you invited her
to come stay."

Lady Fairchild blushed. "Well, you see, she was not
entirely terrifying. She also understood how I felt
about things, almost as though she must once have
felt the same. And when Lord Fairchild, well, he
wasn't Lord Fairchild then, at any rate when my husband wished to court me and my parents refused because they considered his prospects so uncertain, it
was Miss Tibbles who persuaded them to let me wed
him anyway. For that kindness, both Fairchild and I
shall always be grateful."

"But why did your parents oppose the match? How
could they think his prospects uncertain?" the colonel
asked, in apparent bewilderment.

Lady Fairchild smiled wryly. "He was not the heir,
then. His older brother was. That is why my parents
considered Fairchild's prospects uncertain. Had Harry
not been killed in a duel, my husband would have had
only what his father or brother were generous enough
to give him."

Merriweather managed to look surprised. "Indeed?
Lord Fairchild had an older brother?"

"Yes, of course. Older by twenty minutes."

"Anna! We do not talk about Harry!" Lord Kendall
said sharply.

At the colonel's look of inquiry, he softened his
voice to explain, "Black sheep of the family, you see.
Got himself killed in a duel, as she said. Embarrassing
to talk about him, even if he was my son."

The colonel immediately looked at Mrs. Merriweather and she looked back. He nodded almost im-
perceptibly and she felt yet again the joy of knowing

she had aligned her life with that of a man whose
mind was so in tune with her own. This brother, Lord
Fairchild's twin, was the one they both most wanted
the family to talk about and now she set about per-
suading them to do so.

"As I recall, your son killed his man, too. Had either man survived, the one who did would have had
to flee the country."

There was almost a questioning note in her voice
and it was Richard Avery who answered her.

"Oh, there were plenty of witnesses to see and note
that the wounds were fatal in both cases."

The Earl of Kendall, however, had had enough.
Rather testily he said, "Yes, well, it did not come to
a question of either man fleeing the country. And now
I should like to forget the matter entirely."

"Yes, of course."

Matters were kept light from then until the end of
the evening when the entire party retired. When they
were alone in their room, however, the Merriweathers
could not help but speculate.

"What if he did not die after the duel?" the colonel asked.

"I have thought the same thing," Marian replied
gravely, "and I must allow it is my belief that his
survival is the likeliest explanation for all of this. But
the earl is not the only one to say there were witnesses. And I have seen the grave."

The colonel snorted. "Anyone may bury an empty
coffin and who would think to dig it up?"

Marian paced about the room. "Yes, but I spoke of
it to Sir Geoffrey and he had already had the same
thought. He checked and the coffin is not empty. Of
course," she added cautiously, "after all these years
one cannot tell a great deal about the body buried
there."

"But the risk!"

The words hung in the air between them. "Tomor-

Chapter 21

As she had every day of Mrs. Merriweather's visit, Lady Fairchild sought out her former governess in the morning. And again she drew her aside into the yellow parlor. But to Marian's eyes, Anna seemed more agitated than usual. It took some moments for Lady Fairchild to come to the point, almost as though she had to gather her courage to do so. When she did, she began without preamble.

"I should have spoken to you frankly before this. Now I have no choice. I spoke with Edward last night. He finally admitted to me that it was his brother Harry who was murdered here and that he did know Harry was alive. But he swears he did not know it until two months ago. That was when the letters began to arrive."

"Letters?"

"Threatening letters. Demanding letters. Harry wished to be paid to stay away. But Edward told him to come home and it seems he did," Anna ended bitterly.

"Did Lord Fairchild kill him?"

"No! How can you think such a thing?"

"Didn't you?"

"He swears he did not."

"I see."

"No, you do not! You see opportunity and secrecy and reason for murder. But it is not so!"

"The man is dead," Mrs. Merriweather said as gently as she could.

"But not by my husband's hand!"

"I pray, for your sake, that it is so," Mrs. Merriweather told her former pupil. "But if not by Lord Fairchild's hand, then by whose?"

"We don't know!" Lady Fairchild cried and the anguish in her voice was very real. "We talked until dawn, Edward and I, trying to guess. But how can we?"

Lady Fairchild paused and spread her hands. It was a moment before she could go on. Mrs. Merriweather simply waited.

"Every person in this house might have had reason enough to wish Harry dead. But even so, I can see none of them murdering him."

"Everyone?" Mrs. Merriweather said with apparent surprise.

"Well, almost everyone," Lady Fairchild amended. "Or so Edward says. He will not tell me why, for he says he cannot, he will not betray secrets. But he says it in such a way that I must believe him. Just as you should know if you can believe the colonel or not when he tells you things."

Mrs. Merriweather nodded slowly. She did understand what Lady Fairchild meant. "Very well," she said. "Suppose we accept as true everything you have said. Why are you telling me these things?"

Her former charge looked at her derisively. "Because I knew you must already have guessed much of it. It has not been so long that I cannot remember how perceptive my dear Miss Tibbles was. How much she saw that one would wish she did not. And I did not wish you to think that it was only Lord Fairchild who might have had reason to wish his brother dead."

She paused and sank into the nearest chair. Her eyes were dark from too many nights with too little sleep and her face mirrored the dismay she felt. Her voice became low and husky as she finally went on.

"This was a happy household for most of the years I have lived here. Beginning just days after Harry's apparent death. Until two months ago. When the letters began. Edward has had some but I am guessing others in this house have had letters as well. And then, after the night of the ball, when I am certain Harry pretended to be Edward, it became much worse. I think he must have found an opportunity to taunt several members of the family. Even I, though I did not guess it at the time. He asked me if I ever thought about what it would have meant if Harry had not died. I thought him in a contemplative mood. I did not guess it was Harry himself behind the mask asking."

Mrs. Merriweather nodded. "Yes, I remember the mood the day after the ball. I should guess you are right. Harry," she said severely, "was not a nice man."

"He deserved to die, all those years ago!" Lady Fairchild said fiercely. "I am not sorry he is dead now, only sorry that it must have happened at the hands of someone I have come to consider family."

It was Mrs. Merriweather's turn to pace about the room. "You must know that when the inquest is held, it is likely Fairchild will be accused of the murder."

"I do know it," Lady Fairchild said, her voice scarcely above a whisper. "And though I have come to love his family, if it is a question of Edward or one of them, I should rather we find the true murderer than let him be accused."

"And I should like to know because no matter how justified, I cannot be comfortable with someone who has now killed twice," Mrs. Merriweather countered dryly. "For we cannot forget the stranger. For my part, I wish we knew who he was."

Some distance away, Sir Geoffrey was saying precisely the same thing. "I wish to know who the man was! Have you had any luck in discovering it?" he asked the Bow Street Runner standing in front of him.

"Oh, aye, sir. That's why I be here. Went back to the duel, I did, just as you asked. Found where 'is lordship was took when 'e was shot. As many years as it were, I found the inn where 'e was took. And the private 'ospital where 'e was took arter that. To recover like. Only 'e didn't. Not for some time, 'e didn't. And when 'e did 'e was mad like. 'Ad a keeper. And a 'ouse all to 'is own. 'Cept 'e was chained. Like they do in Bedlam. Only 'e slipped 'is chain. Killed a man doing so. Took up wif another 'un. Laid low, they did, for a nice long while. Last they was seen they was 'eaded for 'ere. I'm guessing t'friend played least in sight while 'is lordship went up to the 'ouse. And was killed. Got worried, 'is friend likely did, and went looking for 'im. From the description I'd say the second body wot was found were that of 'is lordship's friend."

Sir Geoffrey nodded. He rubbed his chin. "I am of the same opinion. So Lord Fairchild wasn't killed? But wounded in the head so severely that he lost his wits."

"For years, they said," the Bow Street Runner confirmed. "Even at the last 'e 'adn't gotten back all that much. But enough to know 'oo 'e was."

"And thus he came back to claim his inheritance."

"Looks like 'e was murdered to prevent that," the runner added.

Sir Geoffrey looked at him sharply. "Perhaps. Perhaps not. There could be other reasons. I've learned a great deal these past few days, that tells me Lord Fairchild was not a pleasant man."

"No, that 'e wasn't," the runner agreed. "Everyun 'ired to look arter 'im came to 'ate 'im, they said. And couldn't keep a female near nor in the 'ouse. Even if 'e was chained. 'Course maybe 'e was like that afore the shooting, too."

Sir Geoffrey's eyes widened at that. "It would explain a great deal," he said thoughtfully.

The runner waited as the magistrate stared for some time at the wall. At last the runner grew restless enough to ask, "What was you wishing me to do next?"

That brought Sir Geoffrey out of his reverie. He sighed. "Unfortunately, there is not a great deal you can do. The inquest will be held tomorrow and it will be my unpleasant task to accuse the one man who seems most likely to have done this. And the devil of it is that if he did, he has my profound sympathies."

In the kitchens, the colonel was sipping tea with Mrs. Breen, and Damford was regaling them both with a story or two he had heard about the late Lord Fairchild.

"We all knew he would come to a bad end, sir," Damford concluded, shaking his head. "Even when the earl purchased his colors for him, we knew it wouldn't last. And now this stranger, appearing like he did, dead in the library! It's like there was a curse on this house, it is. Or on the family. And that magistrate, poking about. Wanting to make trouble for the family, is what I say. They ought to refuse to speak to him. We have, the staff, I mean. But no one asks our advice, of course."

"Of course," the colonel said in a sympathetic voice. "Why, when I think of the slights poor Mrs. Merriweather endured as a governess!"

He paused to shake his head. "I shall always say it serves them right to have to let her into their homes as a guest, now that she's my wife. Teach them to treat their staff with such thoughtlessness in the future!"

This, however, while raising Mrs. Merriweather in their esteem, for now they could understand why she would presume to visit as a guest in the household, caused them considerable unease. Damford and Mrs. Breen looked at each other. Damford spoke first.

"I won't say this family mistreats any of us, sir."

"No, of course not," the colonel agreed obligingly. "They simply don't see you. Don't notice you at all, much of the time. Means you've heard a great deal they've no notion you overheard, I'll be bound."

"Well—"

"Damford hears more than I do," Mrs. Breen made haste to say, so as to draw the colonel's attention back to her. "On the other hand, the maids and such hear more than he does and they're not shy in telling me."

"I'll bet they are not," the colonel said, leaning toward her. "You seem such a motherly sort I can see they'd want to confide in you."

Mrs. Breen looked a trifle flustered, as well she might. The colonel really did have a very nice smile, she thought to herself.

Damford cleared his throat. "The maids might have overheard more than I have," he said slowly, "but I'll be bound the master never confided in them as he has in me."

The colonel nodded wisely. "Mrs. Merriweather said he'd likely have done so and that I should ask you." As Damford started to stiffen, he hastily added, "M'wife wants to help, you see. She has a fondness for Lady Fairchild. And she said the staff would know things. She also said most likely his lordship would have confided in you, because he would know you would understand, you having been with the family so long, and all."

"That he did, sir," Damford allowed, thawing a bit. "Not that I feel I could betray his confidences."

"Shouldn't dream of asking you to," the colonel replied, with an innocent, wide-eyed stare. "Only meant that you might know something that would help his lordship."

Damford hesitated, then slowly shook his head.

"No. It would be as much as my place is worth to tell you what the earl said. I'm sorry, sir, I can say no more. And you, Mrs. Breen, oughtn't to say anything either."

The colonel, too shrewd to press the point, rose to his feet, his head whirling. The earl? He had meant Lord Fairchild, but of course the confusion was natural. He wondered, though, what it all meant.

He realized that both Damford and Mrs. Breen were regarding him with an anxious stare. Hastily he said, "I thank you. Both of you. I am sorry to have intruded on your work. But ever since I was a boy, you see, I have been more at home in the kitchens than anywhere else. The result of a cook who spoilt me ridiculously, I daresay."

Mrs. Breen smiled indulgently and even Damford's lips twitched, though he was too well trained to betray himself. Still, as the colonel headed for the stairs back to the main part of Kendall Hall, his conversation with the staff had given him a great deal to think about.

The entire family, it seemed, was privy to the scene that took place between Sir Geoffrey and Lord Fairchild in the entrance hall. Lady Fairchild was among the last to get word of what was happening and to come down.

What she saw gave her a severe shock, for there was no mistaking what was going on. There was no mistaking what it meant when Sir Geoffrey informed her husband that the inquest was set for two days' hence and he was to presume that he might be bound over for trial afterwards.

Had he been anyone ordinary, Anna knew, he would already be under arrest and on his way to jail. The look on his face, his unnatural pallor, told her only too well that he understood.

Suddenly Lady Fairchild could not bear to see her husband looking so distressed. She pushed everyone

aside and took her place by his side. She rounded on
the magistrate and said, "You would put your time to
better purpose, sir, if you bent yourself to the task of
finding the true murderer rather than abusing my
husband!"

Sir Geoffrey reddened but he kept his voice remarkably calm, remarkably gentle as he said, "I will allow
for the natural feelings, the natural loyalty of a wife,
Lady Fairchild, but I suggest you prepare yourself for
the worst." He paused and turned to Lord Fairchild.
"Remember, sir, the inquest is set for the day after
tomorrow. I suggest that you put your affairs in
order."

And then Sir Geoffrey turned on his heel and left
the hall, followed by the constable. Lord Fairchild
bent his head and wildly Lady Fairchild looked around
at the servants, who refused to meet her eyes, and the
family, who were no better. Lady Winley had a look
of smug satisfaction on her face and Catherine merely
looked bored. Only Mrs. Merriweather met Anna's
eyes and with a look of such sympathy that Lady Fairchild almost felt herself undone.

Suddenly, as the crowd dispersed, Anna saw her
daughter. Pamela ran to Lord Fairchild and hugged
him. "It will all come about, Father. It must! I know
it must!"

Lord Fairchild smiled at Pamela and patted her
shoulder, but there was no hope in his eyes. Nor
would he look directly at Anna. When he walked
away, it was with rounded shoulders so unlike his
usual proudly erect carriage.

The Earl of Kendall looked so pale he might faint,
and Pamela moved to his side to support him. But he
was made of sterner stuff than his son, and at Pamela's
touch his color returned and he glared at Mrs.
Merriweather.

"You!" he said with loathing in his voice. "If it were

not for you and your meddling and your assistance to Sir Geoffrey, none of this would be happening!"

The former governess studied him a moment, as though choosing her words with care. Lady Fairchild held her breath, but when Mrs. Merriweather spoke, she merely said, "There would still be two dead men."

"Would there? Or would there only be one?" the earl countered. "How do you know the second was not the result of your meddling? In any event, what do I care of dead bodies? I care about my son! And now he is about to be arrested." He paused and turned to Anna. "I hope you are still pleased that you invited this creature to stay, for I am not."

Then, before either woman could answer him, the earl turned and strode away, his back rigidly erect. Anna looked at Mrs. Merriweather, who could only shake her head, her eyes patently full of sympathy.

The hall seemed to quietly become empty, only Anna, her daughter, and Mrs. Merriweather still standing there.

"Well," the former governess said briskly, "we've not much time to solve this riddle. I had thought Sir Geoffrey more perceptive but then he has not stayed in this house as I have been doing. I think the colonel and I had best bend our minds to the purpose."

"Yes, but can you do so?" Anna asked. "Solve the mystery, I mean?"

"I shall do my best."

It did not satisfy, this answer. But before Pamela or Lady Fairchild could say anything more, Julian Deerwood was announced. The two older women, by silent mutual consent, retired from the entryway as well.

As for Julian, he took one look at Pamela's face and drew her outside where, as he told her softly, "We may talk freely without fear that anyone shall overhear."

Pamela nodded and allowed him to lead the way. He took her, as she expected, to the rose garden, where they both knew they would not be disturbed. And he insisted she sit before she tried to tell him what had occurred. She did so as succinctly as she could. All the while, Julian held Pamela's hand. It was only when she was done that she lost what little composure she had managed to gather to herself.

"So the inquest will be held very soon?"

She nodded, too overcome to speak. A tear trickled down her cheek and he wiped it away with his thumb.

"I shall be there," he said. "Surely they will rule death by persons unknown."

"I wish it were so," she said. "But I fear they will blame Papa. Sir Geoffrey warned him to expect that he may be bound over for trial."

There was nothing to be said to that and Julian didn't try. Instead he put his arms around her and held her close as she cried until there were no more tears within her left to cry.

"It will come about," Julian said fiercely. "It must!"

"I wish it were so," Pamela whispered, "but I cannot see how."

There was a sound behind them and instantly Julian moved away from her. He let out a sigh of relief when he saw it was Richard. "Any word?" he asked.

Richard shook his head. "No. I've escaped the house because I can't bear all the gloomy faces anymore. So," he said, looking from one to the other, "you are stepping beyond the bounds of propriety. Grandmother would not be pleased to know it. She fancies a brilliant match for our Pamela. But then she fancied a brilliant match for all of us and her plans have come to nothing, thus far."

"Do you mean to tell her?" Pamela asked with an anxious frown.

"Me?" Richard snorted. "No, I've no wish to cause you trouble. Or to ruffle her feathers yet again. She's as likely to strike out at the nearest person, which would be me, as call the two of you to account for it."

"Then why do you bother telling us how she feels?" Julian asked.

Richard waved a careless hand. "Oh, because I thought it would be amusing. Why else? But I've no malice in me. Not like Uncle Harry. I, for one, am glad he's dead and think the whole world better for it. No, I am no Harry. I'll even make my apologies for disturbing you. And leave you to your solitude."

Then, as they watched, he walked away as easily as he had come. Pamela frowned at the sight. To Julian she said, "There is something very strange about Richard these days."

"I should think so! Anyone who indulges as freely as he does, this early in the day, would act strange. Yesterday he was so drunk he was ill. Today he's merely bosky. But then, it's early hours yet."

Pamela looked incredulously at Julian, then at Richard's retreating back, as though trying to decide how much to believe. Finally she leaned against Julian and said, "One more person to worry about. Is everyone going mad?"

"Not you and not me," Julian assured her. "No matter what, I shall protect you and together we may weather any crisis, no matter how terrible."

Wanting to believe him, Pamela rested her head against his chest and pretended, at least for the moment, that he spoke the truth. Still, she could not help warning him.

"Grandmama won't be happy about this."

Julian grinned down at her. "She doesn't frighten me and I won't let her frighten you. It's your grandfather I'm more concerned about. I know how much he takes your welfare to heart. Indeed, at your uncle's funeral he said that he would do anything to protect you."

Pamela looked up at Julian. She blinked. "He said he would do anything to protect me?" she repeated.

Julian nodded, puzzled.

Pamela slowly pulled away. "Why would he say such a thing then?" she asked.

"I don't know," Julian said, trying to remember. "But I know he spoke of failing with others in the family and he did not mean to fail with you." When she did not speak, he touched her shoulder. "Pamela? What is wrong? Why do you look so distressed?"

She looked up at him, then, her eyes large and worried. "Julian, do you remember the day of my uncle's death? How my grandmother kept to her room?"

He nodded and she went on, "I went upstairs to talk with her. We spoke of the dead man. She seemed to feel more grief for him than anyone else, as though she knew who it was and it was someone dear to her. I don't know how or why I found the courage, but I asked her if she knew who had killed him. And, Julian, she told me that she was sure it was someone who believed himself or herself to be protecting the family!"

They looked at one another. "But surely you cannot think your grandfather, Lord Kendall, could be a murderer?" Deerwood said at last.

Pamela looked away, then back at him. "It would seem impossible and I am reluctant to think so and yet it makes a bizarre sort of sense. Julian, I think perhaps we ought to go find Mrs. Merriweather and tell her about this. She will know what to do, how to sort it all out."

He looked doubtful for a moment, then abruptly he made his decision. "Yes, of course, you're right. We must tell someone and better someone not of the family. Someone who has been here, observing everything, but who has no reason to believe or disbelieve whatever we might say."

Together they turned and headed for the house. One of the footmen, in answer to their question, told them that Mrs. Merriweather had last been seen heading for the library. They went to find her.

Chapter 22

Lord Kendall moved through the hallway slowly. His heart pounded in his chest. He felt as though he had aged ten years when he heard Sir Geoffrey's words today. The man was very likely going to arrest his son. Edward! And there was very little he could do about it. Maybe it had been a mistake to kill the second man. But what choice had he had? Money wouldn't have kept him silent for long.

Not that anyone was likely to guess the truth, even so. But it worried him that Edward was going to be blamed. Oh, he was unlikely to be convicted, but the suspicion alone would hurt him horribly.

Dash it all, why had Harry survived that duel anyway? He'd been meant to die, ought to have died, in a sense *had* died. And the world had been better for it. But then he came back. Came back and threatened everything.

Who might guess? Or worse, who might find evidence to make it seem that Edward, or someone else, had done the deed? Immediately an image of the governess came to mind. The former governess, he corrected himself. Pamela had repeated some of the things she said and it was worrisome.

The woman saw too much, understood too much, he thought. He could not allow it to continue. He should have stopped her permanently when he had the chance. Except that then he had not yet come to think of himself as a murderer. Only as someone who

had done what must be done. But now, with two dead,
what difference did it make if there was a third? But
he must be certain that it happened at a time when
no one else could be blamed.

The rustle of skirts in the hallway alerted him that
someone was coming. He started to turn to see who
it was. But then he didn't need to turn. The woman's
voice told him who it was.

"So. There you are," Lady Gwendolyn said in her
shrill, unpleasant voice. "Hiding, I suppose. Afraid
someone will ferret out your secret?"

"My secret?"

"Oh, yes. You were careless. Most careless."

"What do you want?"

"What else, my dear brother, but money? Money
so that I can leave here. Money so that I can set up
on my own. Money so that no one will ever look down
on me again. Father should have settled something on
me before he died so it's only right that you should
do so now."

"And for that you are willing to overlook murder?"
Lord Kendall demanded.

He couldn't help himself, he found it funny. Lady
Gwendolyn did not. Anger clouded her voice as she
said, "Why not? Were it not for Harry, I should have
had the life I wanted to have. It seems only simple
justice that his death should bring it to me at last."

He understood. He really did. He even felt sympathetic. Lady Gwendolyn was right to blame Harry. She
always had been. It was a pity he didn't like his sister.
Because if he had liked her, he would have helped
her leave long ago. Or he could let her go now. But
Lord Kendall had never liked her mother, his father's
second wife, whom she greatly resembled, and he did
not like blackmail. No, there was only one option now.
Slowly he turned and smiled at her.

"Of course, my dear," he said, in his gentlest voice.
"Why don't you come into the library and I will open

the strongbox for you. Would you care for some brandy first? It will help to steady both our nerves as we settle the plans for your departure."

Colonel Merriweather saw the couple enter the library and he hurried to catch up. There was a matter or two he wished to speak to the gentleman about and he had not yet had much of a chance to talk to the lady. Marian would no doubt be pleased with him, he thought, that he took such initiative.

They had not closed the door entirely and so he opened it, pretending not to have noticed anyone enter before him. He was in time to see the Earl of Kendall pouring brandy for himself and Lady Gwendolyn.

"Oh, er, sorry to disturb you," Colonel Merriweather said with affable good humor. "Didn't know anyone was in here. Door was partway open, y'see."

The Earl of Kendall regarded him with patent annoyance. "Was there something you wanted?" he asked.

Merriweather waved a hand. "Thought I'd find a book to read. Not much in that line, in general, but I've heard you've such a fine library here, y'see, I thought I ought to take a look."

"Yes, well, perhaps you could look later?"

"Certainly, certainly."

The colonel turned, as if to go, and then paused. With his hand on the door he said, "Oh, er, by the by, I meant to ask you if your son Harry ever purchased his colors. Thought I remembered a fellow by that name."

The earl set down the bottle of brandy with a distinct thud. He made no attempt to hide his anger as he said, "Purchase his colors? Oh, yes, my son tried the military. And failed abysmally, as you must know if you recall him being there at all."

Merriweather coughed. "Well, yes, er, but I wasn't certain it was the same Fairchild."

"Not certain?" The earl's choler was high. "How many Lord Fairchilds do you think there are in England?"

The colonel spread his hands. "Well, but it's been so many years that I could not help but wonder if my memory was playing tricks on me. I might have mistaken the name or the title or even what his career had been. So I thought I would ask."

The earl blinked at him. "Why on earth should you care? What the devil difference can it make to you who or what my son might have been?"

"Oh, er, nothing. Nothing at all," the colonel said hastily. "My lamentable curiosity, you see."

"Yes, well take your damnable curiosity and get out of the library and preferably even my house!"

Merriweather judged it best to press no further.

"Wait. I shall go with you," Lady Gwendolyn said, surprising both men.

"Why?" the earl asked, staring at her hard.

She smiled at him but it was not an amused or gentle smile. "I believe I have things I wish to discuss with the colonel."

"What can you possibly have to say to him?"

"Oh, this and that."

"Well, here, perhaps I was too hasty. Why don't the two of you sit and have some brandy and talk here?" the earl suggested.

Lady Gwendolyn shook her head. "Oh, no, I think I should like to talk with the colonel in private."

"Well, at least have some brandy first."

Mrs. Merriweather moved down the hallways of Kendall Hall growing more and more uneasy. Where on earth was Andrew? If only she hadn't stopped to talk so long with Lady Fairchild. Mind you, it shouldn't matter. There should be no need to worry. After all, it was not as though anyone would have any reason to attack him. And yet Marian did worry. Some instinct told her that she ought to find him and find him as quickly as she could.

It was not, however, a trivial task. Everyone she asked denied seeing him. And then, just as she reached the main hall, one of the maids admitted to seeing the colonel enter the library.

"He's there with the earl and with Lady Gwendolyn, I believe, ma'am," the girl said with a curtsey.

Mrs. Merriweather's eyes widened. "I see. My dear, please find Lord Fairchild and send him to the library at once. Or Mr. Deerwood. Or even Damford. Anyone you can find."

"Yes, ma'am."

Never mind that the girl clearly thought she was wanting in wits, never mind that it might be a foolish, useless request. Mrs. Merriweather could think of nothing else to do, no other way to bring help. Help she dared not wait to arrive. Not if her suspicions were correct. Not if she was right that the murderer had grown even more unhinged with Sir Geoffrey's visit and his threat to arrest Lord Fairchild.

She hoped her suspicions were flawed but she dared not risk it. She wished she had told Andrew what she was thinking, but hadn't because it had seemed so impossible. Now she realized she had been foolish to take the risk.

Like the colonel, though she could not know it, Mrs. Merriweather pushed open the door to the library without knocking. There she found Lord Kendall and Lady Gwendolyn and Andrew all drinking brandy and engaged in what appeared to be amiable conversation.

At the sight of Mrs. Merriweather, there was complete silence. Then Andrew said, his words slurring slightly, "Yes, m'dear?"

Mrs. Merriweather forced herself to speak calmly, to keep from clenching her fists, to smile, to pretend to a want of wits, none of which was real. But she hoped it would be good enough to fool the others. In her pocket was the small pistol the colonel had given her. She hoped she would not need to use it.

She took a step toward the colonel and let herself frown. "Indulging, Andrew? At this hour?"

"It is only brandy," the earl said with a chuckle. "Would you like some, Mrs. Merriweather? It is a dreary day outside and this will warm your bones."

Mrs. Merriweather threw back her head. "No! That is, I thank you, Lord Kendall, but no. I do not indulge this early in the day, no matter what the occasion. But it would seem my husband is not as prudent."

She willed him to look her in the eyes and read the warning there. But Andrew only looked at the earl and said, in confidential tones, "You see? A tyrant! That's what she is, a tyrant!"

"Perhaps you ought to go with her," the earl said with careless ease.

The colonel nodded. "P'rhaps," he agreed. "Lady Gwendolyn, do you wish to stay here or with us?"

But she had the oddest look upon her face and did not at once answer. She tried to rise and sat back down again. "I feel very strange," she said.

"Tell Damford to call a physician!" Mrs. Merriweather told her husband.

"I—"

"He is going nowhere. Nor are the two of you," Kendall said, rising to his feet, a pistol in his hand.

As they stared at him, he looked at Mrs. Merriweather. "Go over to the wall," he said. "There by the fireplace. Press the leaves as I tell you."

She did not argue. Not yet. Better to seem cowed and helpless. Still, her hand moved closer to her pocket even as she did what he said. This time when she pressed the carved leaves and flowers as he directed, a door sprang open.

"My word!" the colonel exclaimed.

"I knew about the secret cupboard, of course, but never guessed that this existed as well," Mrs. Merriweather said, staring at the secret doorway in fascination.

"Harry knew all about it," Lady Gwendolyn said, from behind them.

"So he did," the earl agreed. "Found it as a boy and used it often. Always for the worst of purposes."

"Just as you mean to do?" Mrs. Merriweather asked, slipping her hand into her pocket and closing it over the pistol.

"You leave me no choice!" Kendall exclaimed in exasperation.

"But Lady Gwendolyn is your own sister!" the colonel protested.

"Half-sister," the earl replied curtly. "I greatly disliked her mother and the feeling was quite mutual, I assure you. Lady Gwendolyn takes after her mother."

For a moment that stunned them all into silence, for what was there to say to that? But then Mrs. Merriweather rallied and tried again. She wished to keep him talking, not only to learn what he might say, but also until Lord Fairchild or Damford or someone arrived. She could not be certain, after all, that she could draw out her own pistol faster than he could fire his. So now she pressed him.

"It will do you no good. You might have escaped discovery had you stopped with your son, Harry," Mrs. Merriweather said quietly. "Or even with the stranger. But three more of us dead? How do you mean to hide that?"

The earl looked at his sister bitterly. "Had she not decided to blackmail me, I would never have needed to do this. And then you, sir, stumbled in upon us and she meant to confide in you. And then you, madam, had to intrude. Does no one believe in privacy anymore?"

"It would seem not," a voice said from the doorway of the library.

They all looked to find Julian Deerwood and Pamela standing there, side by side. "You cannot do this, Grandfather," she said as she took a step into the room. "You must not do this."

"But I did it for you," the earl told her, his voice soft and pleading. "Harry would have taken away your father's title. But not before he did horrible mischief. And he meant to do to you what he did to Daphne."

Lady Gwendolyn gave a gasp of horror. The earl looked at her. "Don't pretend you didn't know," he said in an exasperated tone. "You must have."

She shook her head. "Daphne would never tell me what was wrong. Did she tell you?"

A snort of disbelief. "Tell me? No, but he did. Harry made it part of his threats."

Mrs. Merriweather had her pistol out and behind her now, but she did not yet display it. Not while the earl seemed inclined to confess. Not until she could move a little closer to where he stood.

"What threats?" she asked.

But the earl ignored her. He took a step toward his granddaughter. "He was here the night of the ball, pretending to be your father. I saw the way he danced with you at the ball. The way he held you, touched you, looked at you, Pamela. He would have attacked you, sooner or later, as he attacked her. I couldn't allow that to happen."

Pamela had gone very pale. "I thought it was my imagination," she whispered.

"Oh, no." The earl shook his head and took another step. "I assure you, my son Harry was precisely that sort of monster."

"He apparently pawed Miss Winley as well," Mrs. Merriweather added quietly.

"And ruined Richard as well as my husband," Lady Gwendolyn threw in, not troubling to hide the bitterness in her voice. "He took my husband to gambling dens and encouraged him to wager away every last penny he had. He took my son to a brothel when he was but fourteen and encouraged him to every excess after that. In the end, all the Avery lands had to be sold just to pay off the debts so that I and my children were left penniless. But I didn't know about Daphne. Harry was a monster, there can be no doubt about that."

"But I thought he was killed in a duel before I was born," Pamela protested.

"Everyone thought he was killed then," the earl said slowly.

He sank onto the nearest chair and his eyes took on a faraway look, but not so faraway that anyone dared charge him while he held the loaded pistol in his hand. Even Mrs. Merriweather waited, curious to hear what else he might say. After a moment he went on.

"They carried him to an inn. The physician pronounced him done for. But he didn't die. He lingered for a while and then began to recover. But not entirely. His mind, never very strong, was even more disturbed after the duel, for the shot struck him in the head. He was violent, out of his mind. When word was brought to me, I arranged for him to be cared for privately. He was guarded every minute of the day and night. I was to be told if he showed any signs of recovering his senses. Slowly he did, but I could not risk him coming back here. Not when his nature was still the same."

Again he paused and briefly rubbed his forehead. Then he looked at them, anguish patent in his eyes. "By then Edward was acknowledged Lord Fairchild. And he carried his duties well. He lived out no scandal, hurt no one. I could not let Harry come back in his place. So I ordered him kept restrained. And for a time it sufficed."

The earl paused and stared into the empty fireplace. His thoughts seemed very far away. Eventually, however, he began to speak again.

"A few months ago there was a fire. No one can say how it started. It gave Harry the chance he needed to escape. He began to write. Threatening notes. Teasing notes. Some demanded money. Some said he would return no matter what we did. He came back the night of the masquerade. There was no way to capture him then without the secret being revealed. And then he disappeared again for a day or two. He left us a letter taunting us with how easy it had been for him to create mischief. He said he would come again. When he did, I was waiting for him. I knew that sooner or later he must come through this secret doorway. When he did, I killed him and I do not regret it, no matter what the cost."

"And the other man?" the colonel asked.

"When he discovered Harry was dead, he tried to blackmail me." Kendall paused and looked at Lady Gwendolyn. "I do not like blackmail," he said. "Not even from my sister. Unfortunately, you are too much like your mother, my father's second wife."

Then, while they still stood there, stunned by all these revelations, Kendall raised his pistol. Now Mrs. Merriweather raised and pointed hers at him. But she never had a chance to speak, for the earl suddenly put the pistol to his head and fired.

"Oh, my God!" Colonel Merriweather cried and leapt to his feet.

Lady Gwendolyn slid to the floor, whether in a faint or something worse.

"Get a physician!" Mrs. Merriweather told Julian, who was closest to the door.

Pamela was already on her knees cradling her grandfather. Mrs. Merriweather rested a hand on her shoulder and, when the girl looked up, said, "Had it not been for you and Mr. Deerwood, he might have succeeded in killing us. It was for your sake that he did not."

Pamela took it for the gesture of comfort it was meant to be. She pretended not to notice the pistol Mrs. Merriweather held. Instead she turned back to her grandfather. Whatever he had done, there was a part of her that did, that always would, love him.

The shot, of course, had drawn the rest of the household, family and guests. Lord Fairchild had finally been found. And Damford.

Mrs. Merriweather looked at the major domo and said, "You'd best send for Sir Geoffrey." Then she turned to the family and added, "I think it would be wise for everyone to wait in the drawing room. I shall come as quickly as I can."

They went. All save Lady Kendall. She was the last to enter and she was the last to leave. When the others were gone, she advanced far enough into the room to look down at the earl and then she spoke to him, almost as if he were still alive.

In a voice that was as cold as ice she said, "You murdered our son. Whatever Harry did, he was still our son and you kept him from me for almost twenty years. Maybe if you had let me, I could have loved him enough to change him from the man he was to the one he should have been. But you kept him from me. It is only fitting that now you should be dead, too. If I were not such a coward, I would have murdered you the day you killed Harry. But you have done the task for me and for that one small favor I am grateful."

And then the countess turned on her heel and strode from the room.

The colonel looked at his wife. "You took your time drawing your pistol," he said.

She looked at him placidly and replied, "We were not, it seemed, in imminent danger and I wished to hear everything he would tell us. It is not, after all, as though we would have any other way to find out for certain how and why he killed his own son and the other man. Or what he intended."

Merriweather nodded. He looked down at the body. "Pity. Still, I daresay you were right to do as you did. To give him the chance to shoot himself. Far better than if you had to face an inquest for his death. Better for everyone, all around, I daresay." He paused, then added, "He saw your pistol, you know, right at the end. He knew there would be no chance of escape."

She nodded. Only now, when all the danger was past, did she begin to tremble. It was then, with a muffled curse, that the colonel reached out and gathered into his arms the woman who was so dear to him.

They scarcely noticed when the door opened and Lady Fairchild peered into the room, saw them, and quietly closed the door again.

Chapter 23

It was too much to hope that matters could be resolved without scandal and indeed Anna, Lady Kendall now that her husband had inherited his father's title, confided to Mrs. Merriweather that she did not think it possible.

"We must hope you are wrong," Marian replied. "And you know I shall stay as long as you need me."

But the new countess shook her head. "You have a husband and child who need you even more and I can see that he is eager to carry you back home."

Before Marian could answer, Sir Geoffrey was announced. He asked to speak with the former governess alone.

"Please let her ladyship come with us," Mrs. Merriweather countered. "This touches her far more than it touches me and I'll vouch for her discretion."

Sir Geoffrey hesitated a moment, then consented. "Very well."

When they were in the small room that had become so familiar to both the magistrate and the former governess during the investigation, he cleared his throat, looked at both women, and said, "I think I have contrived to avoid a major scandal."

At their exclamations of delight he held up a hand warningly. "I'm not saying his lordship was right to murder his son," he added sternly. "I'm not saying that at all. But the late Lord Fairchild made himself hated hereabouts and for good reason. It's no loss to us that he's dead. And I'll even admit I think it for the best Lord Kendall took his own life as well. Now we'll have no need for a trial. The inquest is over and a verdict found that the earl took two lives and his own while of unsound mind. He'll not have to be buried at the crossroads."

"Thank God, and your efforts, for that small measure of mercy!" Anna said in gratitude.

Sir Geoffrey looked at her and nodded. He paused, then said, "Perhaps you had best go join the others, ma'am. I'll be there shortly to take my leave of your husband, the new earl. And the dowager countess as well. I really do need to have a moment in private with Mrs. Merriweather."

"Of course."

They waited until she was gone then Sir Geoffrey looked at Mrs. Merriweather. "You've not had an easy time of it here over the past few days, I'll be bound," he said. "They'll not have thanked you for discovering the truth. Except perhaps for your former charge. She's grateful, no doubt, that you saved her husband."

Mrs. Merriweather regarded him with a sardonic smile. "I know such families too well, Sir Geoffrey, to have expected any other treatment than what I have received. They will be pleased to see the back of me as soon as may be. All except, as you say, Anna and her husband."

"Perhaps," he agreed, "but whatever they may think, I should like to say that it has been a wonder and a pleasure to have known you, Mrs. Merriweather."

She thanked him and watched him go. She waited until she thought he must have had sufficient time to make his farewells before she went in search of the family. It was time to take her own leave but there were things that must be dealt with first.

*　　*　　*

Julian held Pamela's hand. "I still want to marry you," he said.

She felt unaccountably shy as she looked up at him. "And I should like to marry you."

"Then come, let us go speak to your father."

The entire household, it seemed, was gathered in the drawing room. Lady Winley was there with her daughter, and both were discussing with the colonel the best road back to London. Lady Gwendolyn was there with her daughter and son. The new Earl of Kendall and his wife, Anna, were present and so was the dowager countess. And right behind Mrs. Merriweather came Mr. Deerwood and Lady Pamela.

"I presume now that Sir Geoffrey has brought us word the investigation is concluded that you and the colonel mean to leave, Mrs. Merriweather?"

"Yes, we do," Mrs. Merriweather replied gently.

"Oh, but—" Miss Winley broke off in some confusion.

In answer, Mrs. Merriweather looked at Richard Avery, who rose to his feet. He came over and took Catherine's hand. "We may as well announce now," he said, "that Miss Winley and I are going to be married as soon as I can procure a special license."

"What?"

That one word echoed around the room as almost everyone reacted with shock. Lady Winley rose to her feet, her face very pale. "Nonsense!" she said. "You cannot marry Mr. Avery. Your father threw him out of the house when he asked. We told you he is merely a fortune hunter. You cannot so far forget yourself as to marry him. Neither your father nor I will countenance such a thing!"

But Richard was not in the least daunted. "I am very sorry you find the notion so distasteful, Lady Winley, but we are going to be married." He paused, took a deep breath, then added resolutely, "Your daughter is increasing. I have spoken to my uncle and he has agreed to allow me to become steward for his Scottish estates. He has also made a settlement on me that will allow me to support Catherine."

"You are going to Scotland? My daughter is increasing?" Lady Winley echoed in dismay.

"Mama, I shall be happy, truly I shall. Now that we can tell you," Miss Winley said.

"But he only wants your money!" she wailed.

"That may once have been true," Richard said quietly, looking down at his bride-to-be with the tenderest smile upon his face that anyone had ever seen. "But I have come to truly love Miss Winley and I promise I shall make her happy. Certainly I shall try."

Nearby, Julian Deerwood cleared his throat. "If we are to make announcements, then perhaps it would be as well for me to say that I should like to marry Lady Pamela and that she has said she should like to marry me."

There was an edge of defiance to his voice, but Mrs. Merriweather could have told him he would not need it. Not when the new earl and countess must remember so well how it had been for them when her father opposed the match on the grounds that it was not grand enough.

The dowager duchess, however, was not so sanguine. "I'll not have it!" she snapped. "The match is not nearly good enough."

Her son smiled at her. His voice was gentle but implacable as he said, "Yes, but it is good enough for me and that is all that matters. Mr. Deerwood, my daughter is very young and I cannot countenance a wedding until she has had a Season. But I do not doubt that your affections will prove true, and if that is so, then I shall make no objection to the match. It is my dearest wish that you may both be as happy together as Lady Kendall and I have been."

As he spoke, the new Earl of Kendall took his

wife's hand in his and she blushed as though she were a young girl again. The dowager duchess snorted. "Next I suppose you will tell me that Daphne means to marry a pauper!"

It was Lady Gwendolyn who answered. "No. Daphne and I mean to travel to Italy. We will take a house in Venice or Florence or perhaps even Rome. And there we will build a new life for ourselves."

The dowager countess was speechless at the news but only for a moment. "You can't go!" she said with relish. "You've no funds!"

Lady Gwendolyn shook her head. "Edward has been kind enough to settle a portion on each of us. We will not be rich but we will manage."

A bleak look came into the dowager's eyes. "It wasn't supposed to be this way," she said. "You were all supposed to marry well. Kendall and I were supposed to have had many more years together. You were all supposed to listen to our advice. Instead you mean to go your own way, all of you." She rose to her feet. "I shall not stay and listen to any more of this nonsense!"

They watched as she left the room. It was Mrs. Merriweather who spoke first. "It will take some time for her grief to ease. Particularly as she mourns both a husband and a son."

"And what will you do now?" Anna asked her former governess.

Mrs. Merriweather smiled and looked at her husband. "The colonel and I must return home. I have already stayed far longer than I meant to. But I am so glad to have seen you and to have been able to be of service to you again."

The new Lady Kendall rose and came over to her former governess. "And I am so glad you came," she said. "I don't know what we would have done if you had not. No, nor how we would have managed through all these difficult days."

And then, to the scandalous astonishment of everyone present, they embraced. "I shall always be there if you need me," Marian told her former pupil.

"And I, here, if ever I can be of service to you!" Anna replied, grasping Mrs. Merriweather's hands tightly.

A few more words were exchanged between them and then the Colonel and Mrs. Merriweather left the room to pack. Indeed the entire party separated, emotions running too high for them to remain in one another's company.

Mr. Deerwood and Lady Pamela sought refuge in their favorite place, the rose garden. They seemed oddly shy with each other. It was she who said, watching his face very carefully, "I was shocked to learn of Miss Winley and my cousin Richard's attachment!"

"Their impending marriage, you mean," he said, meeting her gaze squarely.

She swallowed and nodded. "Yes, their impending marriage. And the baby they are expecting."

"It is shrewd of your father to send them to Scotland," Julian said. "By the time they return to London, no one will be quite certain when they met or married or anything else. And thus there will be no scandal."

Pamela nodded again. "You, you are not terribly upset, are you, Julian? Your heart is not broken?"

He looked down at her. What he said now would be, he knew, the foundation of their life together. Somehow he must make her understand how he felt and why. He took her hands in his and led her to the bench, where they sat side by side.

"I did not know, until I saw you with Miss Winley, how much you meant to me. I did not understand how much I valued your sweetness, your gentleness, the bond we have shared between us. But when I did, then I knew that I wanted you by my side for the rest of my life. Because I love you. And I always will."

As he finished speaking, he raised her hands to his lips and kissed them. Still, she did not at once reply. Instead, for a long moments she searched his face. Then she pulled one hand free and touched the side of his cheek.

"I think I have always loved you," she said. "Though it is only when you told me about Miss Winley that I knew my own heart. But I was so afraid you only asked me to marry you because of the murders. Because you felt you must stand by me."

He colored and wished he could say she was mistaken but he would not begin with lies. "I did," he said in a low voice she had to strain to hear. It grew stronger as he went on. "But only for a very short while before I understood that my own sentiments had undergone a change. That it was not Miss Winley I wanted but you. And that it was not duty which drove me but affection."

"You do not think of me as a sister, then?" she asked teasingly.

"A sister?" he echoed, taken aback. "Good God, I do not!"

And then, drawing her close, he proceeded to show her, in a most satisfying way, that his affections were far warmer than a brother might feel toward a sister.

The new Lady Kendall, coming in search of her daughter, beat a hasty retreat at the sight of Mr. Deerwood and her daughter embracing. Instead she went in search of the new earl. She found him in a parlor that was to be renovated to be his new study for, as he put it, he would not have a moment's peace if he tried to read in the library and he dashed well would have a new one!

"Anna, is something wrong?" he asked, coming forward when he saw her standing in the doorway, an odd expression on her face.

"No, Edward," she replied, stepping into the room

and closing the door behind her. "Nothing is wrong. Nothing at all."

And then, before he could ask any more foolish questions, she put her arms around his neck and pulled his head down so that she could kiss him. The moment he realized what she was about, he tossed down the book he held and embraced her fully as fervently as she embraced him. And that was how a scandalized Damford found them, a short time later, when he came to announce dinner.

As the carriage rattled on its way, taking them back to their home, the Colonel and Mrs. Merriweather regarded each other warmly. Little Elizabeth was in the other carriage, safely being seen to by Marian's maid so that they could have some privacy. Privacy that the colonel was very grateful for. He had something to say and he thought Marian would take it far better if there were no one else to hear.

"*Hrrrmph,*" Andrew said, clearing his throat. "While I do, er, understand, Marian, why you felt you could not desert Lady Fairchild, that is to say Lady Kendall, when the bodies were found, I, er, do hope you don't mean to make a habit of such things."

"Make a habit of such things?" She looked at him in astonishment. "How on earth could one make a habit of such things?" Her eyes narrowed and her voice became tart as she said, "I scarcely think many of my former pupils are going to invite me to visit, and even if they did so, you cannot think any more are likely to be encumbered with dead bodies lying about the place!"

"No, er, of course not. It's just that, well, dash it all, Marian, you had me worried! I don't know what I should have done if anyone had attacked you."

Mrs. Merriweather grew very quiet. This was not, perhaps, she allowed to herself, the time to tell him about being bashed on the head in the library. It was one detail she had been careful to omit when she told him what had gone on at Kendall Hall.

So now she merely patted his hand and said, "My dear Andrew, I scarcely think you need worry about that! I promise you I shall spend the rest of my life in quiet contemplation, if you wish."

"Quiet contemplation of what?" he asked with some suspicion.

Mrs. Merriweather looked at her husband with wide, innocent eyes. "Why, quiet contemplation of whatever you wish, of course, my dear."

And that nonsensical answer received precisely the snort of derision it deserved! But since she followed it by placing a hand over his and tilting her face up for a kiss, the colonel soon had other matters to divert his mind. It wasn't until miles later, as they stopped for the night, that he recalled her answer and his own disbelief in it.

By then, however, Mrs. Merriweather had had ample time to think of even more ways to divert his attention, particularly now that they had a bedchamber in which she could show him what she had thought up. And to their mutual delight, for the rest of the evening she did so.

Author's Note

I had great fun resurrecting Miss Tibbles from my Westcott series. She is one of the most formidable characters I have ever created. For all her promises to Colonel Merriweather, I somehow doubt this will be the last adventure Mrs. Merriweather encounters. So don't be surprised if she appears again in the future.

Look for news of upcoming books at my website: http://www.sff.net/people/april.kihlstrom

I love hearing from readers. I can be reached by E-mail at: april.kihlstrom@sff.net
Or write to me at: April Kihlstrom
                       PMB 240
                       532 Old Marlton Pike
                       Cherry Hill, NJ 08053

Please send an SASE for a newsletter and reply.